Table Of Contents

Bad Roommate

Moist

Moist. Wet. Steamy.

That's what I'm paid to get women every night.

Horn them up and then send them home to their spouse or vibrator, whatever their satisfaction tool of choice is.

My job is done when they walk out the door of the club giggling, flushed, and excited.

It's just a bonus I get paid extremely well to make it happen.

Dancing isn't my lifelong dream. It's a means to an end.

At least it was until she came into the club with a group of her screaming, drunk friends.

Shy and reserved, she caught my attention straight away as she tried to keep her eyes diverted from the action on the stage.

My intention was to open her up and pull her from her shell.

I didn't expect for her to flip my whole f*cking world upside down.

Contact Information

Description:

Never room with a playboy. Words to live by. Unfortunately, I seemed to have missed that memo. When Carrington Anderson shows up on my doorstep applying to become my roommate, I'm immediately shook. He doesn't remember who I am, but I sure as hell remember him.

He'd broken my heart and been part of the reason my high school years had been complete and utter torture for me. I still dealt with the emotional and mental damage high school had inflicted upon my psyche.

Now ten years later, a hundred and fifty pounds lighter and adorned with more tattoos than a sailor, I wasn't even close to being the same girl I'd been back then. The girl I used to be died a long time ago.

I thought I could resist his charms this time, but I was sorely mistaken. As we got to know each other all over again, I feared he'd destroy my heart a second time around.

Bad Roommate

By

Terry Towers

Copyright Notice

Bad Roommate

by Terry Towers

Published by Terry Towers

Soft and Hard Romantic Publishing

Cover by Sylvia Frost

www.thebookbrander.com

Printed in Canada

1st Edition

Chapter 1

Felicity

Oh my God! I groaned inwardly, sinking back into the overstuffed, navy plush sofa. My pure black cane corso mastiff, Misty, who'd taken up the vast majority of the sofa, lazily opened her chocolate-brown eyes, looking up at me with her head tilting slightly to the left.

"I don't want one either, believe me. But rent in New York is expensive and an apartment that will take a dog your size is even more expensive. So this is kinda your fault - really. We can't afford the bills on our own for much longer. I'm running through my savings quicker than I'd like," I found myself explaining even though I knew she wouldn't understand a word. "Long story short... We need a new roommate."

I sighed. Twenty-eight years old and still needing a roommate. It wasn't where I expected my life to be headed when I graduated from high school. I had dreams of marriage and a baby and the white picket fence just outside the city. But as it turns out, we don't always get what we want in life.

My doorbell rang. Looking down at my watch, I frowned. This Carrington dude was fifteen minutes late for his interview – he didn't give me a last name in his email. Though his email address started with playboy4ever, so I wasn't expecting much – no doubt a douche. Considering only two of the five scheduled for today had shown up, I'd give him half marks for at least making an appearance and not wasting my time. The people I met yesterday were complete disasters.

The buzzer sounded again.

"Yeah, yeah. You're late and now I'm the one expected to rush… Not looking good for you so far buddy," I muttered more to myself than to the dog who didn't bother to join me in the walk across the room and to the intercom.

"Yes," I said, pressing the button and waiting for a reply.

There was a pause and then, "This is Carrington. I'm here to do a meet and greet for an apartment."

Pressing the talk button, I replied, "Come on up. Fifteenth floor, apartment 1521." My index finger lingered on the talk button before hitting the button to buzz him up, just long enough for me to take notice of the fact that I was long overdue to have my nails done, the white gel polish had grown out a solid quarter of an inch. It's crazy how easily you can lower your standards for your looks when you weren't out hunting for a man. Aside from going to the gym downstairs and my daily run, who'd I have to impress, the clerk at the convenience store down the street?

As I waited at the door for him to arrive, I felt a wave of nerves. This had to work out, I couldn't handle many more of these waste-of-time interviews. On the other side of the door, I faintly heard his footsteps coming down the hallway, however, I waited at the door for him to knock and allowed the span of a couple beats before twisting the knob and pulling it open to avoid looking too anxious.

At 5'2, I was always shorter than most other adults but as I swung the door open, my line of sight focused on the broad chest of a man that had to be 6'2, maybe even 6'3. My eyes traveled up his broad chest with a black cotton t-shirt stretched across it, to a handsome face with a couple days' worth of scruff.

That's when it struck me.

I knew this man. Just looking at him made me tremble inside as a slew of old memories I'd rather have forgotten about rushed through my mind. It had been a long time since I'd last seen him, not since high school, but there was a point in time – a long time ago - I'd known him quite well.

"Carrington…" I blinked hardly believing my fucking eyes. "Carrington Anderson? Are you fucking kidding me?" Shaking my head, I took a step back from his massive, sexy as sin body. He even smelled amazing, the intoxicating scent of his cologne drifted to me, teasing my nostrils.

His eyes narrowed as he stared down at me, a weak smile on his lips. "Do I know you?"

I wasn't surprised he hadn't recognized me. I hadn't seen him since high school and I'd changed a lot since then, including losing well over a hundred pounds and dyeing my naturally dark hair to platinum blond. The array of colorful rainforest tattoos littering both my arms were also very new additions. Some would argue my insane need to modify myself had a lot of do my lack of self-esteem through years of mental and emotional torture at the hands of my classmates.

They wouldn't be wrong. I spent a lot of time and money to rid myself of the girl I used to be to become the woman I was today.

It was on the tip of my tongue to tell him who I was, Connie Felicity Boyce. Formally, Connie the Cow as my high school peers had called me. Oh, the good old days. Something held me back though. I'd been going by Felicity Boyce for years now.

Clearing my throat, I took a step back and shook my head. For whatever reason, I didn't want him knowing he used to know me. "Sorry, I mixed up who was coming at what time. I…" Hoping he wouldn't give it much thought I waved him inside, closing the door behind him.

Did I really want to live with this asshat? He was part of the reason my high school life had been so horrible. He crushed me and it hadn't even fazed him.

My eyes scanned his broad back and dipped lower. He had one seriously fine ass. Sincerely, you could bounce a damned nickel off it.

Misty stretched, placing her front paws onto the floor and slowly pulled herself from the sofa, casually crossed the living room to greet Carrington, her bobbed tail wagging happily for some pats – traitor.

"Big dog." Reaching down, he gave her a few pats on the head.

"Yes, she's getting old so she's not very energetic anymore – not that she'd ever been all that active to begin with."

His gaze shifted from the dog to me and he smiled. His smile lit up his entire face, an amused twinkle in his dark blue eyes.

I'd always admired how gorgeous his eyes were, an alluring deep sapphire blue. The type of eyes you'd lose yourself into if you didn't watch yourself.

Connie the Cow… Connie the Cow. A voice at the back of my head chimed in – mocking me. He'd been one of those bullies. He'd never tormented me directly, but he never attempted to stop the ridicule. Had he tried to stop it then, they would've listened to him. My senior year of high school would've gone much differently – all he had to do was say stop. But he hadn't. He hadn't because then people might've remembered we'd dated the summer before our freshman year of high school and judged him for it.

Connie the Cow.

So he didn't, he allowed the torment.

As much as I would've liked to simply let it go and move on, my high school years had affected me in ways that lingered a decade later. Those years had broken me mentally and it had taken a long time to rebuild myself.

"I can live with that." He gave Misty another pat on the head before surveying our surroundings and nodding. "Nice place. The ad said it was a two-bedroom?"

"Umm. Y-yes…" Giving myself a mental kick, I led him past the kitchen, small dining room area and into the living room. Crossing the room, I opened the blinds. "We've got an excellent view of the park." I shrugged. "It's not Central Park or anything, but it's nice nonetheless if you like to jog or to relax with a picnic… Or whatever. The greenspace is nice either way." Placing my hands on my hips, I glanced up at him. How long would it take for him to recognize me? Despite all the physical changes in me, there was a very good chance he'd figure it out on his own – eventually. He'd just need to come across a yearbook or old high school photo. Luckily, I hated the way I looked back then so all photos of me were tucked away in albums or boxes in the closet and were never looked at.

"Great." His eyes scanned the horizon. "Loving it already."

"I'll show you the extra room. It's not huge or anything. Just a room." Leading him to the bedroom situated across from mine next to the bathroom, I opened the door and stepped aside allowing him entry.

As he swept past me his elbow lightly grazed my breast, sending a little shiver through me. Inhaling sharply, I took a step backwards distancing myself from him. Fuck, maybe the problem was I hadn't been laid in what felt like forever. Had to be for me to get shivers over Carrington fucking Anderson.

Why the hell I was showing him the apartment instead of kicking his ass out was beyond me. It's just the other candidates had been so questionable in more ways than one. At least he seemed normal.

He's a prick, but at least he's a normal prick.

Carrington nodded as he slowly turned. "This would do. Room for a queen-sized bed and a dresser. What more could a single guy ask for, right?"

"Suppose so. Do you expect to have plenty of company?"

He grinned his gaze pinning me. "Would that be an issue?"

"I wasn't planning on getting a male roommate. The only reason I'm considering it is because my last roommate slept with my boyfriend so figured a male roommate would be a better fit."

"I'm sorry to hear that. For what it's worth, the guy was a fool to do that to a woman as stunning as you are."

Heat rose to my cheeks. "Thank you. I appreciate you saying that."

"Did it all work out? With your boyfriend? Still together?"

Cocking a brow up at him, I laughed. Though the chuckle was more over my stupidity than the hilarity of the situation. It hadn't been funny at all, just another blow to my fragile ego.

"Yes, it's going great," I answered dryly, rolling my eyes.

"I bet. So single and strictly monogamous, that's your deal?"

"It's not yours?"

He shrugged. "Yeah, well. I like to keep my doors wide open. Life is too short, ya know?"

Crossing my arms over my chest, I eyed him for a minute. "Well, we're nearing thirty, there comes a point when finding your happily ever after should be a priority."

"A couple years to go before thirty, just saying."

"If that helps you sleep at night. Let's chat for a few minutes if you don't mind?" Spinning on my heel, I left the room and settled myself onto the sofa waiting for him to follow behind.

This wasn't high school. This was adulthood. We were on even ground. In fact, I had the advantage because I had something he wanted and needed – a place to stay. Apartments in this area were hard to come by. The realization still hadn't eased me as my gaze followed him as he made his way across the room to sit next to me.

"What do you want to know?" He shot that sweet, sexy smile at me again. I remembered that smile, it made me swoon back then and a decade later, it still had an effect on me. "I'm an open book."

Just kick him out. This is insane. Get rid of the asshole, the voice in the back of my mind chimed in. *It's not like you'll be able to live with him!* Having him here brought back bad vibes. Vibes I didn't need, especially when I'd tried so hard to move on.

But I ignored the voice.

"What do you do for a living? Should I expect a parade of women here? I'm not overly comfortable with a hoard of women coming over each night. I value my privacy. I'd rather not have the hassle of keeping all of the names straight."

His head jerked back and a roar of laughter erupted from him. "Just because I'm not the kind of guy that relishes the thought of a serious relationship doesn't mean I'm a player."

When I cast him a skeptical look. "That's not what your email handle says."

Chuckling, I could've sworn I noticed a hint of a blush appear on his cheeks then fade just as quickly. "That email was made a long time ago. I just never bothered to get a new one, less embarrassing one." When I raised a skeptical brow he continued, "I promise, I'll be discreet."

"And occupation?"

"I'm an artist, though a struggling one. I just started a gig tattooing at a shop not too far from here. The money isn't great yet, which is why I'm looking to share a place." He looked down at my heavily tattooed arms. "Nice ink by the way."

I looked down at the tattoos that I hardly knew were there anymore, they were a part of me now. I nodded. "Thanks. The artists were amazing to work with." Clearing my throat, I straightened on the sofa. "This is temporary then?"

"No. If the situation works with us then I'd like this to be a permanent thing. I'm not looking for Miss Right or anything of the sort, so moving out isn't something I have any intentions of doing anytime soon."

My eyes scanned him for a moment. He'd always been a good-looking guy, but the additional years had given him a more chiseled, mature look. His jawline was sharp with a dimpled chin. I could only imagine how many women he had lined up. I'd bet his phone was filled with girls' numbers. Hell, even though I hated him, I still felt an attraction towards him. It didn't help that he'd worn a cologne that drew me to him with its fresh, woodsy scent.

In fact, flashes of how good it'd felt when he'd kiss and hold me all those years ago came racing to the forefront of my mind. I'd foolishly thought it would be forever. But I suppose many girls feel their first boyfriend and love would be the one. Part of the teenage girl daydream. It was never reality, but at the time it was easy to forget that.

Damn. Sliding back on the sofa a tad, I attempted to distance myself from the temptation.

"Look… Felicity…" He placed a hand on my shoulder, the heat from his hand radiating through me, making me feel all warm and cozy inside. "I suspect you have reservations. I get that, so I'll level with ya. I need a place and it's not easy to find a good roommate. I've had my share of bad ones. I need quiet to work on my art and being new at tattooing, I'd be at the shop more often than not. I won't eat all your food and you'll hardly know I'm here most of the time."

He looked so earnest, nothing like the egotistical piece of shit I'd once known. People changed; they changed all the time. I changed over the years. Maybe I shouldn't fault him for what happened to me in high school. We were adults now. Fuck, he didn't even recognize the new me now. It had been nearly ten years. Maybe I just needed to let bygones be bygones and move on, that's what mature adults did.

I needed a roommate sooner rather than later and he was the best of the bunch I'd interviewed so far. It'd be stupid to allow petty teenaged issues to get in the way of paying the bills and passing up on a potentially good roommate.

Slowly with a tingle of apprehension in the back of my mind, I stretched my hand out for him. "You've got yourself a new roommate, if you want to move in that is."

A smile crept across his lips as he accepted my hand, his large hand wrapping around my considerably smaller one giving it a firm shake. "Would moving in tomorrow be too soon?"

My heart accelerated at the thought of him living here so soon. It was frightening and exhilarating at the same time. Tomorrow wouldn't give me much time to clear my head of the fact that I'd be living with the first boy that broke my heart. But at the same time, having additional time meant I'd obsess over the situation for longer than necessary. I just needed to treat this like a Band-Aid, one rip and straight off. Forcing a smile to my lips, I replied, "Not at all. Roomie."

Chapter 2

Carrington

One of the biggest pains in the ass of life would hands-down be moving. Damn. But at least I had a place to live now and it was a decent little apartment near the train station. What more could a guy ask for? The chick that lived there was certainly hot. If it wasn't for the fact that I couldn't afford to be kicked out, I would've taken a shot with her at the meet-and-greet. Just the thought of getting between those silky legs of hers had me instantly hard. Fucking embarrassing how much of an effect she'd had on me. I would've thought I'd matured past boyish hormone induced hard-ons by now.

Evidently not.

Shaking off the thought of her, I climbed the old, creaky wooden stairwell to the second floor of the motel in Newark, New Jersey. The doors to the rooms were all outside access and I was partially surprised the stairs and second floor walkway were still together and holding weight. This place was straight out of a movie – horror movie that was. I was sure there were by the hour rooms in the joint where hookers and addicts hung out. I'd seen quite a few shady characters lurking about, I'd just done my best to keep my head down and ignore them. Being that I was a particularly big guy, people tended to ignore me for the most part.

I'd been living in a motel and commuting to work in Manhattan every day for the past couple of weeks. It wasn't ideal and my meager number of belongings had taken up a good chunk of the space in the tiny room, but it was a place to lay my head. I'd convinced the owner of the motel to take a back tattoo from me in exchange for the room since I was severely short on cash. I hadn't been joking when I'd said I was a starving artist. This wasn't exactly the life I'd expected for myself at this age. My naive adolescence had expected I'd end up being some hotshot football player making millions.

Inserting the key into the door lock, I twisted it and the lock disengaged, allowing me entry. The room had a faint musty smell that quickly greeted me, reminding me of the lack of upkeep the place had received as I entered, flicking the switch to the light just inside the room. The light over the bed turned on with a faint buzzing sound and the fan over the bed began to rotate, making a slightly creaking noise as it rotated.

"One more night." I murmured to myself. I didn't have a bed or dresser currently. I'd have to make an IKEA stop tomorrow before moving my things. Closing the door behind me, I was impressed by the cleanliness of the room despite the age. The owner's daughter cleaned all forty rooms in the motel and did an amazing job. She was a damned hard worker and I respected her for that.

A small grin spread across my lips as I remembered my night with Sophia. The least I could do was show her a good time after how well she cared for my room. The motel was most definitely full-service. For a split second, I considered giving her a call and asking her to come over for one last bit of fun, but quickly dismissed the idea. I had a long day tomorrow and for some strange reason, the thought of being with Sophia didn't excite me like it had in the past.

Pulling my t-shirt up and over my head, I tossed it onto the cracked brown leather armchair by the door. The dirty clothing pile on the chair had become rather large at this point. The washing machine at the motel was broken and had been that way since I'd moved in. Thankfully I'd be out of here tomorrow, another couple of days and I'd have to turn my boxers inside out to wear them.

Selecting what I'd planned on wearing tomorrow from the remaining clean laundry, I picked up the large white, net laundry bag and stuffed all my dirty laundry inside until it was nearly full.

Grabbing the remote to the television, I flicked it on, not so much to watch what was on, but for background noise. I wasn't one for solitude. I'd always loved having people around, but this motel room just wasn't the place for entertaining guests and I'd couch surfed enough before moving into the motel room that I was pretty sure I'd outlived my welcome with my buddies – at least for now.

It wouldn't take long to get everything I owned packed up and neatly stacked, ready to go when the moving van pulled up in the morning. It worked out cheaper and easier just to hire a van with movers than it was to rent one myself and then deal with the logistics of coming back for my car.

Stripping out of the rest of my clothing, I tossed them into the dirty laundry bag and made my way into the bathroom. The bathroom was basic and there wasn't a bathtub, which was a bummer for me. The feminine side of me relished a good, warm, relaxing bath on occasion. I enjoyed bath salts, bombs and scented candles – the whole works and I really missed that luxury. I'd give the place credit, it had amazing water pressure and the shower had a large, square head that pelted the skin nicely almost like a massage.

Pulling the shower curtain adorned with an anchor aside, I turned the tap on, adjusting the water temperature until it was perfect before stepping under the stream of water.

A soft groan escaped my lips as I closed my eyes and let my head fall back savoring the feel of the water blasting me. As the water slid down my body, I went through the plans I had for the next day. Rooming with a girl would be different. I'd had roommates before, but never a chick. The idea always seemed – complicated. I loved women, and women tended to have an attraction towards me, so to keep things simple, I'd always made it a rule to steer clear of female roommates.

But… There were times when a person had to adjust the rules and guidelines they set for themselves and take a chance. This would be one of those times.

Squirting some body wash into my hand, I lathered my chest and abdominals, moving southward. Before I knew it, my hand was around my rapidly growing erection. I was only slightly surprised by this occurrence. Felicity had been as sexy as fuck when I'd met her, she came off as cold and in control, but I'd noticed a vulnerability in her gaze.

What was she hiding? What secrets was she guarding and holding tight to her perky, yet ample chest? Would she ever trust me enough to let me into her world?

I moaned as my hand's grip on my dick tightened ever so slightly and I stroked it. Up and down, slow at first envisioning my hand belonged to the woman I'd move in with tomorrow. Damn, it felt so good. The muscles in my back and neck clenched as I stroked myself harder.

In my mind's eye, I envisioned her before me, on her knees in the shower at my feet with her large blue eyes staring up at me as her small, soft hand worked my dick and balls with expert ease.

"What do you want?" she'd ask, a devilish gleam in her eyes.

"You," I'd groan, my jaw clenching.

"Doing what?" she'd answer, even though she'd know very fucking well what I wanted. She wouldn't wait for me to respond before adding to my torture. Lowering her head to the tip of my dick, her tongue would lash out, sending a jolt of pleasure through me.

Sliding my hand into her damp hair at the back of her head, I'd urge her closer longing for her mouth to engulf me fully.

She'd resist for a moment or two wanting the tension to build until I begged her for it.

As her free hand grasped my balls, she'd finally put me out of my misery, taking my cock fully into her mouth. She'd moan softly around my dick sending sweet vibrations up my shaft. I'd groan with her as I thrust softly into her mouth.

My heart rate would accelerate until I practically heard the throbbing of my heart in my ears as I thrust against her, working with her hand and mouth. We'd work in harmony as the sensations flowed through me each pump, bringing me closer to that sweet release.

Looking down at her I'd watch my dick appear and disappear from between her lush lips while the water glistened and slid down her body. "Felicity," I'd groan as the tension within me increased to painful heights. "Slow down... Fuck, slow down."

But my request would be greeted with a little throaty chuckle as she doubled her efforts, her hand on my shaft working harder as her other hand started to lightly tug at my balls.

"Oh sweet fuck!" I'd groan out loud as I'd begin to thrust harder into her mouth until she was no longer giving me head, but I was full out fucking her mouth. She wouldn't mind. She'd love it, keeping up with my pace.

"Stop or I'll blow my wad between your lips!" I'd warn, not slowing down my hand fisting tighter into her hair.

She'd moan a little louder this time, granting me permission.

Images from my meeting with her today flashed into my mind; her blue eyes, her tattoos, the cleavage peeking out from under her low-cut shirt and that beautiful, soft round ass. A final image appeared of her once more, on her knees before me in the shower enjoying my dick and that became my undoing.

My hand pumped my cock one final time and I groaned loudly, my head falling back against the cold, wet tile of the shower as a stream of my cum shot out, painting the wall of the shower before me, to be cleaned away by the water cascading down the tile.

Leaning back, I sighed, my heartrate slowly going back down to normal as my dick gave one more shot of cum before slowly depleting in my hand.

"Dammit," I groaned, releasing my dick.

What in the hell had I gotten myself into?

Chapter 3

Felicity

Why was I nervous? It was moving day and he'd given me the first and last month's rent up front. It was a good thing, or at least that's what I'd kept telling myself, but there was a feeling in the pit of my stomach that kept nagging at me. He wasn't an idiot, he'd see me without make-up, no colored contact lenses in and with my natural hair color eventually. What then? It had been a decade, but he'd figure it out soon enough. The extreme weight loss and years that had aged me may not keep my true identity masked.

Even with me going by my middle name, he'd eventually see a letter that used my first name or some random photo I'd leave out by mistake and when he thought long enough about it the pieces would fall into place.

But did it really matter? A voice in the back of my mind chimed in. *We're not in high school and we're different people. Just let the past go, surely he has.* But I knew I couldn't. I had confidence now, as a new person. The person I used to be was long dead, but if he knew who I used to be then that chubby, nerdy girl everyone used to tease and torment would be resurrected.

The buzzer sounded and I yelped, nearly tumbling from the sofa.

Dammit, I was too on edge for my own good.

Placing my phone on the coffee table, I hurried across the apartment and pressed the intercom. "Yes."

"Delivery for Carrington Anderson," a voice on the other end stated.

"Come on up." Pressing the button, I unlocked the front door for him. Once certain the delivery people were inside the building, I opened my front door and then ushered Misty into my bedroom, closing the door behind her. Normally she was indifferent to strangers and had no desire to leave the apartment without me, but she still managed to get in the way at the most inopportune times.

Turning at the sound at the door, two delivery men appeared with a cart piled down with boxes. "They can all go in that room." I gave them both a smile pointing to the bedroom with the door wide open in anticipation for its new occupant.

"Thanks," the larger of the two said, barely looking in my direction as he and his partner proceeded into the room, piling the boxes in the center of the room and quickly leaving without another word.

Seeing the boxes belonging to my soon-to-be roommate made it all feel extremely real. Much more real than I wanted it to be as the fear of what would happen sunk in. Was there any way I could get out of this and save face? There wasn't, I knew that. I'd made an agreement with him and his stuff had already begun to arrive. It wouldn't be fair to him. Good or bad, I'd made the decision and now I had to lay in the bed I'd made.

A knock came at the door. Spinning to face it, I stared for a moment. The knock repeated followed by, "Felicity? You home?" It was Carrington.

I gulped and nodded. "Y-yes." Taking a deep breath in, I stepped forward, grasping the door handle, giving it a twist. Forcing myself to smile, I gave him a nod. "Good morning – roomie." Stepping aside, I waved him in.

Taking a step back, he grabbed the dolly he had sitting off to the side, tilted it back and then rolled it past me, into the apartment and straight into his room. "I've got a number of loads to bring in. If you could leave the door open, I'd really appreciate it."

"Yeah, of course." I watched him as he unloaded the dolly, neatly stacking the boxes in the far corner as I chewed at my inner cheek. "Do you need a hand?"

"No." He turned around and wheeled the empty dolly out and into the little foyer. "I'm good. I'm better at doing this on my own. I'm very particular on how I like things, besides it's not all that much." Exiting the apartment, he hesitated just outside the doorway, turning back to face me. "But if you had something to drink, lemonade or something, that would be appreciated."

"I have apple juice."

He grinned. His smile was so damned sexy, it made my heart do a little flutter. I vaguely remembered how it felt to have his lips on mine. Our very first kiss was at the playground located at the halfway point between my house and his. He'd been pushing me on a swing and when the ride came to a stop, he'd helped me off the swing and kissed me. It had been sweet and tentative. It had been my first kiss and I'd been elated. Sadly, it'd also been one of the last. The relationship had gone downhill extremely quick after summer, once high school started. His popularity soared while mine went into the trash at lightning speed.

It had been one of the happiest, yet most devastating summers of my life.

"You okay?" He asked, shaking me from my thoughts.

Focusing back onto him, his smile had died off and a look of concern etched itself onto his face. Giving a little laugh, I waved a dismissive hand at him. "Of course. I spaced off there for a moment. Sorry."

"Yeah." Giving me an odd look, he disappeared down the hallway.

What the fuck was that? Maybe it'd be better if I just told him who I was. Entering the kitchen, I opened the fridge, located the carton of apple juice and poured him a glass. Really, I should tune him in, but I didn't want to. There was a large part of me that didn't want him to remember because then he'd know what kind of loser I was. I'd worked hard to turn myself into someone others would find desirable – too much time really.

So, I couldn't. Not if I wanted to keep the girl of the past dead and buried.

Was I obsessive over this too much? Yes.

Could I stop myself from obsessing? Not a chance.

Hearing him coming down the hallway, I positioned myself at the entrance of the kitchen and watched as he appeared in the doorway. "Your apple juice is on the kitchen counter."

"Good, thank you. The heat is insane today." Grabbing the bottom of his shirt, he pulled it up, wiping his brow with it. My gaze followed down his body and paused at his abs. Damn, he was ripped. I didn't remember him being that ripped before. He was always an athletic guy, captain of the football team, typical golden boy, but nothing like this.

I nodded. "I can only imagine. Another perk of the apartment is we have air conditioning."

Laughing, he dropped the shirt covering his stomach. "Then I'm already a leg up on my old place. Place was like a sauna at times. I swear, I lost five pounds a day living there."

After he unloaded his dolly, he entered the kitchen and drank down the glass of apple juice in one go. "Once I'm done, we'll have to sit down and discuss how we want to deal with the grocery issue. I'd better warn you now, I eat an insane amount of food. We can work out the food issues later. I promise I won't leech though."

My mind flashed back to when we went to McDonald's together. He'd eaten two Big Macs, a chicken sandwich, large fries and a large Coke. Downed it all and went back for an apple pie. Never gained a pound of fat it seemed, while I gained and gained eating only a fraction of that. But he was heavily into sports – always going – whereas I'd spent my time in my room reading everything and anything I could get my hands on – reading was my passion. Always had been and always would be.

I was able to pull myself from my walk down memory lane before he noticed he'd lost me. "Yeah, not a big deal. We can go shopping whenever. Either split the bill or each have a shelf in the fridge – it really doesn't matter to me."

"Good then." Rinsing his glass out, he placed it on the counter next to the sink. "I'm starving, how about when I'm done with loading up, we order a pizza – on me of course."

I nodded. "Can't wait."

"Hope you like lots of meat." With a wink, he grabbed the dolly and left the apartment.

~*~　TT　~*~

Carrington

There was something very off about Felicity. I just couldn't put my finger on it. Not off in a bad way. Nothing like that, but more in the way of being peculiar. I hadn't been in her room, but after giving the place a good look over, I couldn't find a single picture of her or her family when she was younger. No child photos, no teen photos, not even a graduation photo. Didn't everyone have that? Especially chicks.

I couldn't completely write her off for that though, there might be a hundred explanations for it. But I'd noticed there were numerous boxes of blond hair dye and bleach in the bathroom when I was putting some of my toiletries away, and an array of colored contact lenses. Sure, lots of girls changed their hair color and liked the colored lenses. It just seemed a little off. She also wore a fair amount of make-up. It looked pleasant to the eye, but made me wonder what was under the layer of colors. I swear the woman had more make-up than a professional make-up artist.

Maybe I was just thinking too much into something that didn't mean a damned thing. Lots of women were obsessed with make-up and changing their looks so often, it made you wonder if they were human or a chameleon. I was just trying to get a read for her. Without trying to appear conceited or anything of the sort, normally women gravitate to me, but Felicity on the other hand, didn't seem interested at all. She was pleasant, but very curt.

It was just strange.

Closing the cabinet door under the bathroom sink, I straightened and looked myself over in the oval mirror. Running a hand through my hair, I examined my jaw from both sides, almost time to shave. I generally tried to keep my jawline with a little scruff. Clean shaven gave me a babyface, but if it got too long, it made me look like a damned hillbilly – I had to maintain a perfect balance in between.

Opening the door, I watched Felicity from the bathroom doorway putting the dishes from our pizza dinner away. We were both lovers of meat only pizza, a woman after my own heart. Despite my curiosity about her, I also felt a familiarity in her presence. We hadn't discussed anything in particular while we ate, but I just couldn't help but feel drawn to her. It was nice to know we gelled. With most women, it was either them chattering away non-stop until I shut them up, or we'd sit in uncomfortable silence.

You know you'd met someone special when you could just sit in blissful silence and feel comfortable. Not that I was into her like that. She was definitely my type, but it all came back to not wanting to fuck up something that might potentially be very good. My situation with her was just too good.

"Thought you'd got yourself lost in there," she joked, looking over her shoulder smiling, hearing me cross the living room and into the kitchen.

"Need any help?" I asked, looking around the kitchen knowing there wasn't a thing to help with.

"No, I'm done here."

"This kitchen is spotless." Looking around, there wasn't a single thing out of place. It had to be the cleanest kitchen I'd ever seen. My mother had been a clean freak, but this woman put even my mother to shame.

Planting her fists on her hips, she looked up at me hitting me with a stern look. "And it's going to keep that way. I'm not your momma or your maid."

Chuckling, I put my hands up from front of me and took a step back. "Whoa, settle it down there. I assure you, the man standing here was raised by a woman that valued a clean and tidy house. I wouldn't be so foolish as to mess up a woman's kitchen."

Her aqua blue eyes narrowed at me making me wonder what color was behind those vibrant colored contact lenses, my guess was brown. "And I expect the common area of the apartment to be immaculate as well. What you do in your room doesn't matter to me, I just ask that you respect the common area."

"I promise I can do that."

The tension in her body visibly relaxed and a smile spread across her lips. She gave me a definitive nod of her head that almost made me laugh. "Good then."

Taking a couple steps backwards, I leaned against the wall and crossed my arms over my chest. "So what do you do for a living? You haven't really said much about yourself, or asked me much either?"

She shrugged. "Not much to say really. I work from home. I'm a freelance editor, so Misty and I spend a lot of time alone together in the apartment. Sometimes we work in the park when it's not too crowded with people." She looked over at the dog fast asleep on her fluffy pink dog bed and affection shone in her eyes. "Good thing dogs like to be with their owner twenty-four seven."

"What about dates? And boyfriends?"

With a sigh, she shrugged. "Well, there hasn't been any since the ex. Just not something I'm interested in jumping into again. Not anytime soon. I haven't had the best of luck when it comes to relationships in general. I'm swamped with work now anyhow."

"Right…" I was tempted to dig a little deeper into the whole ex. Maybe the ex was the trigger for the makeover? Lots of women tend to make changes in themselves after a break-up, especially break-ups that cut them deep. It seemed to be a sort of cleansing for them.

"It is," she insisted, giving me a look with a sharpness in her tone that warned me not to press the matter. "I've got some work to get to. I have a deadline to meet. If you don't need any help, I'll get to it."

I nodded. "No, I'm good."

"Okay." She strode past me and into the living room. Grabbing her laptop from the coffee table, she settled herself on the window ledge and flipped open the top.

I watched, still nagged by the feeling of familiarity. It wasn't until she looked up at me with her brows furrowed before I realized I'd been staring. Clearing my throat, I ran my tongue along my bottom lip, thinking of something to ask before I ended up looking like I fucking idiot. "What types of stories do you edit?"

She cheeks reddened and she laughed lightly. "All types really. But I do my best work spicing up erotic romance."

The way she squirmed on the seat told me there was more to it than that. Cocking a brow up at her, I took a couple steps into the room. "You mean sex books."

She huffed, the rosy hue deepening. "I mean erotic romance. And I edit the books, not write them. I'm just elevating the author's stories – that's all. The ideas and content are all theirs. I just make changes and fix technical stuff for the most part."

"Right…" Chuckling, I turned and entered my room, pausing at the door just long enough to call over my shoulder. "I know what that means." My cute little roommate had a spicy side to her – I liked it. Maybe a little too much.

Looking at the stack of boxes needing to unpack, I groaned. Might as well get it over and done with. Ogling my new roommate wasn't going to get the work done.

Chapter 4

Felicity

"Where are you heading?" I gave a startled yelp at the sound of Carrington's voice in my ear. With my hand grasping the door handle I about to leave. He hadn't been kidding when he'd said he was a quiet roommate. I'd barely heard a peep from him since the previous evening. I'd kinda thought he'd gone to work and I hadn't noticed him leaving.

"Out for a jog."

"By yourself?" He nodded to Misty who was lounging on the sofa. "Doesn't she get to go?"

"She's old and has issues with her hips. She doesn't care to jog. I can get her jogging from time to time though. I took her out this morning for a little walk and usually take her before bed for a few minutes. It's as much as she cares to have for exercise."

Releasing the door handle, I took a couple steps back and peeked around him and into his room. Everything was already set up and organized. There was an easel in the corner covered with a white fabric tarp. Beside the easel was a wooden rack of painting supplies. He even had a large, clear, thick plastic mat on the floor under the easel to protect the dusty rose-colored carpet from paint. I had to give him credit, he was very neat and organized.

"You're all set up already. Impressive."

He stepped aside and shrugged. "Yeah, I didn't have a huge amount of stuff. I try to keep my life as uncluttered as possible. House… work… relationships... Whatever it is, I like to keep it simple and uncomplicated."

I didn't miss the mention of relationships. "Relationships, huh? So you're a player then?"

He chuckled and rolled his eyes. "I wouldn't go that far."

"You wouldn't, huh?" I refrained myself from reminding him about his email address.

"Seems you're about to start digging for information, so how about you put that on hold until I get on a pair of jogging pants and then I can join ya. I'll give you all the dirt you want while we jog."

My eyes narrowed as I looked up at him. I didn't care to have people join me for jogs. I still had big girl insecurities. In high school, the popular girls used to run behind me in gym class and make fun of my fat ass jiggling as I did my best to jog along the track. I could still hear their taunts in the back of my mind. It was irrational, I knew that, but many of the scars I received over those teen years had cut deep and were a part of my psyche now.

"I'll buy ya a chili dog at the vendor down the street on the way home." Turning from me, he didn't wait for an answer as he went to his tall five-drawer dresser and pulled open the bottom drawer, grabbing a pair of gray sweatpants. Not bothering with being modest, he undid his jeans and pushed them down, leaving just a t-shirt and pair of black boxers. I turned my head, but not before catching sight of the bulge pressing against his underwear.

"I could've given you some privacy."

"Nah. We're roomies, nothing to hide from me."

Yeah, says you, I groaned inwardly. "I never even said you could come with me. Maybe I enjoy the solitude."

"Your whole life is about solitude."

He had me there.

"Are you decent yet?"

"Depends on what you mean by decent, but yeah, I have pants on now."

Turning to face him, my eyes were immediately drawn to the front of his jogging pants. The large outline of his dick was there, nearly as predominant as when he was wearing just the boxers. I swear, gray sweatpants on men were the equivalent of a push-up bra for women.

Quickly, I turned from him and grasped the door handle again. Opening it up, I sprinted into the hallway, leaving the door wide open in my wake. "You'd better be able to keep up or I'll leave ya in my dust."

A smile spread across my lips as I heard him chuckle and the door close. Instead of the elevator, I opted for the stairs. The elevator would be my prize for the jog on the way back up. Even though I spent a fair amount of time trying to stay fit now that I'd lost my teenage weight, fifteen floors of stairs after a long jog would be the death of me.

As suspected, it didn't take him long to catch up and pass me in the stairwell. He was in as good of shape as he'd been when we were younger. Maybe even better. By the time we reached the bottom of the stairwell and burst into the lobby, I was already breathing hard.

"So where do we go from here?" he asked as we jogged across the lobby and out the front doors. His breathing didn't even appear elevated. "Doesn't matter to me. I just jog until I wear down and then head on home. I take a different route each time just to keep it spiced up."

"You're a wild one then, aren't ya?" he teased, giving me a wink before proceeding left.

"The wildest," I muttered to myself, taking off after him. My life was as boring as they get. I was in New York City for fuck's sakes, but I lived mostly in solitude, he'd called that right.

"If that's the case, you should show me a good time one of these nights," Carrington said as I reached him.

"What are you talking about?"

"You stated you're the wildest. I'd be interested to see just how wild you can get."

Oh damn, the man has fucking Vulcan hearing. "It's called sarcasm."

Sensing I was struggling to keep up with his strides, he slowed his pace. "You do this often."

"Only with special people."

He grinned, cocking a brow at me. "So talk to me about this wild life of yours. Where are you from? The city or are you originally a Jersey girl?"

Shit. If I told him the city I was from – we were from – he'd immediately start to dig and see if we knew some of the same people. But I didn't want to lie either. I knew I'd have to deal with these questions, but hadn't had time to prepare answers to them yet.

"Yeah, Jersey." Maybe I could just keep it vague.

"No shit. Me too. Paterson to be exact."

"Ahh, why'd you move to New York?"

"To tattoo and I was hoping my art would be discovered more easily if I was in the center of it all." We came to an intersection and stopped. Pulling the small backpack from my back, I unzipped it and pulled a water bottle from inside. Twisting off the top, I took a long, refreshing drink as the walk light turned on and we proceeded across as part of a sea of pedestrians. It was close to suppertime, so everyone was getting off work, making the sidewalk traffic even more dense than normal.

"I'm still trying to get used to the crowds."

"How long have you been in New York?"

"Six months. Before the motel I was couch surfing. I tried to jump into my art feet first, but I've realized that tattooing will need to take priority if I want to eat and have a roof over my head. I've killed my savings already."

"Money goes fast living here. I moved here right out of college and had dreams of working at one of the big publishing houses."

"What happened?" Without being offered, he took the water bottle from me and drank the remainder, stuffing the empty bottle back into my backpack that I'd placed over my shoulder, zipping it back up.

"Excuse you! I only brought one."

"I'll buy the next one."

"You gotta learn some boundaries, buddy," I teased.

Chuckling, we didn't go back to jogging when we cleared the intersection instead, keeping a casual walking pace. "We're living together. We're going to get to know each other's bathroom habits, too late to worry about boundaries now. So, what happened with the publishing houses?"

"It was harder to get into than I'd expected. There are jobs, but the good ones are a "know someone and get hired" type of deal. I worked for one for a while but found being a freelance editor full-time gave me more flexibility and ended up paying better. I just have to work a lot. You know what they say about entrepreneurs, you work seventy hours a week to avoid working forty."

"Ever thought about writing your own book?"

I shrugged. "I have, but there's a lot of work that goes into it besides the writing. I'm not sure if I want the headache of all that. I like what I do. Maybe in the future, but it's not a goal for me anytime soon." I kept to myself that I had a novel already complete with visions of a series, but I wasn't willing to share that yet.

He gave me a wicked little smile, making my heart do a little pitter-patter in my chest. "Maybe you just haven't been inspired enough."

Laughing, I pulled the tie from my ponytail which was beginning to sag, and pulled my hair into a tighter ponytail at the top of my head. I hair was cut relatively short but had just enough length to fit into a tiny ponytail. "Why am I getting the feeling you're flirting with me?"

"Now that, Felicity, is your imagination. Everyone knows it's a bad idea to flirt with your opposite sex roommate."

Giving him the side-eye, I began to jog pulling ahead of him a tad. "Right. Or maybe you're just such a big flirt that you don't even realize you do it anymore." Even though it wasn't a possibility to be with him, I couldn't help the part of me that'd started to warm up. I had to remember how he treated me all those years ago. Him flirting with me now was just a reminder of who he was and what he was really like. He was a player when we went to school together and I doubted he'd changed.

"It's called being friendly." He easily caught up to me and met my pace.

"Right."

"Okay, I'm starting to sense you're trying to say something without actually saying it."

I groaned inwardly as I slowed to walking and entered the park. "Okay, how many women do you have on speed dial?" I crinkled my nose up at him as he stood before me.

"I don't know." He ran a hand through his dark hair avoiding meeting my stare.

"Okay." Planting my hands on my waist, I tried to remove the hostility I felt. "If you wanted to get laid, how easy would it be to dial a number and have a girl in your bed tonight?"

"Oh Felicity. Fuck. I guess there'd be a few if I was really desperate for someone."

"How many actual relationships have you been in?"

He looked uncomfortable, the muscles in his neck tightening. "Not everyone is looking for that type of commitment in their lives at our age. What's the rush to settle down? It's like society expects us to be monogamous. Why can't we just enjoy whoever runs across our path and move on?"

Flashes of the night he'd dumped me came to mind, once more rehashing the whirlwind of feelings I'd had back then. He'd broken my young heart that night. It may have been over a decade later, but I wasn't ready to forgive or forget. He wasn't my friend. He was my roommate, that's it. Done and done.

"Like I said before. Player. The world is full of them and you're just one of many." Deciding it was time to head home, I spun on my heel and jogged back the way we came with Carrington trailing behind me. I ignored his callouts for me to stop so we could discuss it further. There wasn't anything to discuss in my mind.

Chapter 5

Carrington

Felicity was an odd one. One minute she was warm and friendly, almost to the point of being flirty, and the next she'd give me the cold shoulder. It'd been going on since I moved in, over a week ago at this point. Maybe I reminded her of her ex and so she was extra guarded around me? I didn't really know. If she'd had any pictures anywhere, maybe I'd be able to judge for myself – but she didn't.

So tonight, I'd get to the bottom of this once and for all.

She didn't seem to be much of a drinker claiming alcohol slowed the metabolism. But she'd mentioned a particular type of vodka cooler that she loved so I'd gone out and found it for her, stopping by the brewery next door to the tattoo shop and grabbing myself a case of some delicious beers while I was at it.

The comment she'd made in the park hit me harder than I'd care to admit. While some men may relish the idea of being considered a player, I wasn't one of them. Sure, I may not be the kind of guy that was ready to settle down, but I certainly didn't manipulate women. I was always very forthcoming about my intentions. The ball was in their court on how they wanted to use that knowledge. Perhaps I'd been in my younger years, but I liked to think I'd matured since high school.

Felicity had a meeting with a publisher today and wasn't due back for another half hour which gave me plenty of time to set the table and have dinner ready for us. She didn't give me the opportunity to buy her that chili cheese dog the other day, so I stopped by Vesario's Pizzeria who claimed to have the best pasta in all of Manhattan and had gotten us a large meat pizza and an order of breadsticks. We'd call it a peace offering.

I was just lighting the candles when the sound of the key being inserted into the lock caught my attention. Giving the table one last look, I was pleased with the result. I'd gone all out even buying a lacy white tablecloth to cover the small, dull wooden table.

The door swung open and Felicity stepped inside. At first, she didn't take notice of the dimly lit room, or the mouthwatering aroma wafering from the food, but it didn't take long for her to turn and immediately spot the food.

There was a glimmer of excitement in her gaze, which quickly turned somber. "Expecting someone?" she asked.

"Well actually, I was expecting you. You didn't give me an opportunity to buy you dinner on our jog the other day, so I decided to bring dinner to you." I shrugged, looking down at the table realizing I may have gone a little overboard. "Vesarios has the best pizza and pasta in town, from what I hear, and I figured you'd be hungry after your meeting… It's not a big deal."

"Oh…"

She had one helluva poker face, I couldn't read her. Impatience quickly got the better of me. "Good? Bad? It seems we got off on the wrong foot somehow and I'm trying to make this right. That's all."

Her stony expression broke and she smiled, the tension she'd held in her body seemed to relax. "No, this is good. I appreciate it. I had a bit of a rough day. It's just unexpected." Shrugging her leather laptop backpack off her shoulders, she placed it on the sofa and came back into the kitchen. "Maybe I've been a bit of a bitch lately."

I shrugged. I wasn't about to dwell on the past and ruin the mood.

While I loved seeing her golden hair flowing around her head as she walked and how the strands caught and reflected the light. I liked how she kept it relatively short showing off her graceful neck and collarbone. It was short enough to give me a nice view of her neck, but long enough that it still looked soft and feminine. She was a smart, talented, beautiful woman. Any man who had a shot with her would be a fool to let her go. Maybe if I could get her to open up tonight, I'd unravel some of the mystery surrounding why she was so guarded.

"Have a seat. I have an additional surprise for you. Just a thank you for letting me move in here. You really saved my ass." Going to the fridge I pulled out one of the coolers and a beer for myself. Glasses were already on the table. Placing the bottles on the table, I sat down across from her.

"Wow." Picking up the bottle, she examined it. "How'd you know this was my favorite?"

Giving her a lopsided grin, I shrugged. "I pay closer attention than you'd think."

I thought I saw a flash of anxiety in her expression. "You okay? This too much?" I motioned to the table that'd given off some serious romantic vibes. "I didn't mean to go overboard."

A smile spread across her lips. "No, it's fine. Better than fine. Thank you."

"How was the meeting?" I asked as we dug into the pizza pie.

Crinkling up her nose, she gave her head a little shake. "Not great." Picking up her glass, now filled with the vodka cooler, she took a long drink, nearly downing half the glass.

"What was the meeting all about?"

With a sigh, she picked up a breadstick and took a bite before answering. "I've been working on a concept for a series of romance novels for a while now and sent them the first few chapters of the first in the series. I'd kept it to myself, wasn't sure if they were good or not."

"That's great!"

"We'll see. I have no reader base. No previous work. I'm an unknown. The only reason I even got the meeting was because I called in a favor. Pretty sure they're going to pass."

I eyed her for a moment. The thought that there was something oddly familiar about her struck me once more. I couldn't quite put my finger on it. It'd been nagging in the back of my mind from the first time we met. I just wished I knew what it was. There was always the possibility that I'd slept with someone who she reminded me of. That was a distinct possibility – I just didn't think that was it.

She drank down the remainder of the alcohol in her glass and then headed to the fridge for a refill. "How about you? How is working at the shop? Do you enjoy tattooing?"

"It's good. Actually better than good. I really didn't think I'd enjoy it nearly as much as I am. I've got a lot to learn and the artists are throwing me all the shit work – flash tattoos, walk-ins, shit that they just plain don't want to do. But on the other hand, I need to pay my dues and work my way up the chain until I start getting my own regular clients. The other day, I had to tattoo a cartoon image of a vagina inside of a heart with a woman's name over it on a dude's inner thigh, really fucking close to his junk. It was fucking weird."

"I bet." A hint of a grin turned up the corners of her lips.

~*~   TT   ~*~

Felicity

As much as I tried to be sympathetic to his plight, the image of his face so close to some guy's cock and balls while working was too much for me to handle, as I erupted in laughter.

"Oh yes, yuck it up. It was great."

Wiping tears that'd formed in the corners of my eyes, I looked back up at him with the grin remaining on my lips. "I wish I'd been there."

"I wish you had been to. Pretty sure I noticed the guy's johnson twitch a time or two. I think he was getting off on it. If I hadn't known any better, then I'd have thought it was some sort of hazing thing for the new guy. The whole shop found it pretty fucking funny."

I cringed even though a smirk remained on my lips. "There will be more you know. I've heard a lot of horror stories from the tattoo artists that have done my work." I looked down at my arms covered in tattoo sleeves of a variety of animals, all bright and colorful. There wasn't much arm space left to tattoo, but I had lots of other spots that needed beautiful art.

"You do have a fair amount of art on yourself." He took one of my dainty hands in his larger, firm ones and pulled the arm closer to him. With his other hand he traced some of the lines of the animals with his index fingers, his gaze fixated on the tattoos as if examining every line and potential blowout.

I held my breath, not wanting to like the feel of his hands on me. Trying to deny the shiver threatening to shimmy down my spine. I didn't want this. I didn't want or need his touch. I hated this man. I'd hated him for over a decade now, but my body betrayed me, making me realize I was lying to myself.

Grabbing my drink, I downed the remainder of the liquid, giving myself an almost instant head rush. The last time I'd gotten drunk was when I had a bender after finding out about my ex and roommate.

Getting up from his seat, he rounded the table to kneel before me. Dropping my hand, he placed his hand on my upper leg instead, which had a large Japanese koi fish tattoo along the outside of my thigh from my knee to my hip. He gently pushed my skirt up my leg, pausing mid-thigh. Looking up at me, I faintly smelled the beer on his breath as he asked, "May I?"

I couldn't speak as the tension within me rose. The apex between my legs dampened my panties. Not trusting myself to speak, I nodded, watching as he pushed my skirt upwards until it was bunched up between my legs and my entire thigh was exposed.

"Amazing work." His hand slowly slipped up my thigh. Looking back up at me he said, "Maybe one day you'll trust my abilities enough to allow me to ink you."

I gulped. God, I needed another vodka cooler. My smile was weak as I looked down at him. I was supposed to hate him. Fuck! Then why did I want him so badly? "I have an entire back that's a blank canvas."

"Most people don't realize what an honor it is when someone trusts you to brand their body for the rest of their lives. For the rest of their lives, they'll have a part of the artist with them. I never quite grasped how intimate it can be – how connecting – especially when you're putting your art on someone who'll remember your connection to it."

I'd never thought of it quite that way before, but he was right. My tattoos meant something to me, they just weren't random markings and I remembered each and every experience and the people who created the art. "I'm sure it doesn't quite compare to other activities."

A lazy smirk crossed his lips. "Such as?"

"Sex for one." Damn, why did I say that? Was I insane? The alcohol was going to my head. The proximity of his body to mine, knelt between my legs, the smell of his cologne as it drifted up to my nose mixed with a hint of beer, it was all toying with my senses and making me say and feel crazy things.

"Sometimes. If the sex is with the right person. Like tattooing, sex can be more or less intimate depending…"

"Depending on what?" My heart raced so damned fast I feared it'd explode through my ribcage.

His deep blue eyes stared into mine. "On the meaning behind it."

I needed to escape to my room. Read an erotic novel or watch some porn, get off and go to sleep. That's what a woman with any type of common sense would do in this situation. He was a playboy – always had been and it didn't appear as though he'd changed much over the years. But I couldn't run from him or pull myself from the spell he'd weaved around me.

Shifting uncomfortably in the chair as the wetness between my legs intensified, I heard myself replying, "And how deep would our connection be? Would it be memorable?" Running my tongue along my lower lip, I waited for his response knowing I'd made a mistake, but no longer caring.

He slowly raised his face mere inches from my body as his head moved up my stomach and between the valley of my breasts until he reached my neck. Moving slightly closer, his lips grazed the side of my neck – so lightly I wondered if it had really happened or was it just my wishful thinking? By the time his lips reached mine – less than an inch away, I felt as though my pussy would explode.

"Would you like to find out?" he whispered.

Chapter 6

Yes… No… Oh My God… YES!

My mind was in turmoil as I tried to sort through the ramifications of what having sex would do to our situation. Good – bad. Yes – no. I didn't want to think, I just wanted to feel…

Maybe it was the mood that'd been set for the evening. Maybe it was the alcohol or maybe it was because it'd been something I'd longed for since I was a teenager. All I knew for certain was that the moment his lips brushed across mine, I was lost.

A soft moan escaped my lips as he slipped a hand into my hair, grasping the back of my head with his large hand, the feel of the slight tug on the strands making my body tremble with need.

Kissing him back with the desire that'd simmered inside me since the day he'd walked into the apartment, I slipped my hands up his chest. My hands came to rest at his shoulders, my fingertips tracing the hard lines of muscle beneath the t-shirt he wore.

The taste of the beer on his lips and tongue as my tongue dueled with his was a faint strawberry and kiwi taste. Pressing myself against his hard body, I moaned softly against his lips.

"Felicity. Why do you have such an effect on me?" he asked, trailing a line of kisses along my jaw.

"I don't know…" I managed to gasp, letting my head drop to the side, giving him access to the tender flesh.

As his lips and teeth reached my neck, shivers raced through me from the top of my head to the tip of my toe, igniting my body and making my pussy throb for him, for closer and more intimate contact.

As the yearning within me increased, so had the need to feel more of him in every way. Grasping the bottom of his t-shirt, I tugged it up. Ending his kisses on my neck, he sat back on his heels and lifted his arms over his head so I could remove his shirt entirely.

"Your body is incredible," I gasped, trailing my fingertips along the lines of hard muscle. As I reached his pecks, he flexed them, startling me. A girlish giggle erupted from me. "Such a goofball," I teased, leaning forward and nipping at his neck just under his chin.

"Not exactly what I was going for, but I'll take it." He grinned, kissing me lightly as he worked the buttons on the front of my sleeveless white shirt, pushing the fabric aside and exposing my chest. Pulling the thin lacey cups of my bra aside, he uncovered my breasts in his view.

Sensing what he was about to do, I closed my eyes and arched my back, pushing my breasts out to him, granting him permission to go further.

He cupped both breasts in his hands, his fingertips gently rolling my large dark nipples into hardened peaks, sending jolts or electric pleasure though me. My fingers dug into his shoulders as the pleasure increased.

Removing his left hand from my breast, he dipped his head and pulled my nipple between his lips, gently sucking it into his mouth, nipping just hard enough to make me moan and squirm in the chair. As he teased and taunted my nipples, switching from one to the other, the desire within me increased. I needed more. My pussy demanded more.

"Carrington, please," I gasped, opening my eyes and looking down at him, hardly believing this was happening. A part of me pushed my reservations to the side for now because all I wanted at that moment was to feel more of him and for the pleasure to never end, be damned the consequences. I'd waited over a decade for this to happen. There was no turning back now.

As if sensing the need within me, he released my nipple and slipped his hands up my inner thigh, pushing my skirt up until it was at my waist, revealing matching pink lace panties and bra.

Allowing my desires to take control, I wiggled my butt to the edge of the chair and slowly spread my legs for him, the coolness of the room teasing my pussy through the wet fabric. "Please," I moaned, placing my hands on his shoulders and pushing him down.

"I love a woman who takes control," he growled, kissing the inside of my leg next to my knee. Slowly, excruciatingly slow, his lips made their way along my inner leg while his free hand cupped my mound, gently squeezing it, using his thumb to tease my already swollen clit.

He moaned a low, feral sound making me quiver. My stomach was in knots, my fingernails digging into his bare shoulders, leaving deep crescent shapes in his flesh. As his mouth reached the apex between my legs, he hooked his index finger into the thin wet fabric and pulled it aside, exposing me to him.

He paused, leaving me yearning. Confused as to why he'd hesitated, I opened my eyes and looked down at him. The look of hunger in his eyes nearly sent me over the edge. "I'm dying to taste you, baby," he growled.

Chewing at my lower lip, I glanced down between my legs. "Then why are you waiting?"

Not needing any further encouragement, he dipped his head again and ran his tongue along the length of my wet slit. I groaned loudly, savoring the feel of his tongue in my most private of places. His tongue hesitated at my clit, flicking and teasing the nub as he thrust two fingers into my lubricated core.

I screamed out at the sudden invasion of his fingers, bucking wildly against his hand, wanting – no needing, more. "More God, more," I begged, fucking his finger and mouth.

"So greedy baby," he growled, his voice thick with lust.

"I am for you."

He continued finger fucking my pussy, rubbing against my G-spot each time they thrust inward. The pleasure was so good. I'd become an expert at making myself come, but it couldn't compare to having a man between your legs worshipping your pussy. My body trembled.

"I'm going to come," I cried out. And just as I was about to explode, he removed his fingers from me leaving me empty and disappointed. Immediately my eyes flew open and I looked down at him.

"Not yet." He hesitated for the span of several seconds. As the seconds passed, my arousal deflated, leaving me in sheer agony.

It was on the tip of my tongue to beg him again when he lowered his head once more, this time thrusting his tongue deep into my core. I gripped his shoulders, rocking my hips against his mouth.

The sensations within me increased, but this time more rapidly than before. In and out, his tongue worked my pussy taking me higher and higher with each thrust. His tongue accompanied his finger as it pinched my clit, increasing the pressure until I bucked and moaned uncontrollably.

I needed to come, as I squirmed against him. I was so close, tight knots squeezed my stomach. I needed release more than I needed anything else at that moment. Just when I thought I couldn't take any more, the tension within me broke and a wash of relief rushed through me, so intense it left me feeling empty and lightheaded. My pussy clenched around his tongue and a rush of my juices greeted his greedy tongue.

He lapped me up as if he were a drying man in the desert, desperately in need of water. Once he was done, he wiped his mouth with the back of his hand as he stood before me, a large, hard bulge pushing against the denim.

"Carrington," I gasped.

"We're not done yet baby." Bending, he grabbed by the waist and hoisted me up and over his shoulder. "Not even close to being done."

"Promise, promises," I teased, hanging over his shoulder, my face just inches from his round hard ass. "Your ass looks amazing in jeans." Reaching down, I grasped both ass cheeks in my hands and gave them a squeeze.

Chuckling, he gave my ass a slap, just hard enough to send a jolt of pleasure through me and reignite the fire between my legs. "You'll be seeing so much more than just my ass in a few minutes."

Entering his bedroom, he heaved me off his shoulder and onto the bed. I giggled, drunk on vodka cooler and lust. It had been way too long since I'd had a man worshipping my body like he was. It felt so fucking good – intoxicating. How I'd gone this long was beyond me?

The room was dark, but the light from the dining room and kitchen gave just enough light for me to see everything I could possibly want to feast my eyes on. Arching my back and reaching my hands over my head, I stretched out on his bed, watching him as he undid his belt and slid down his jeans. The boxer briefs came off quickly after leaving him completely naked at the foot of the bed, his dick standing tall and proud, the head gleaming with pre-cum.

Capturing my lower lip between my teeth, I looked up at him with a coy smile on my lips. "I feel overdressed."

"You do?" He stepped forward, bending down, grasping the waistband of my panties and pulled them down my legs and off.

Spreading my legs for him, I reached between them, spread my labia and stroked my clit while he watched.

"Fuck, girl. You're so damned sexy. You're going to be the death of me."

"Think so?"

"Uh-huh. I know so." Going to his nightside table, he pulled out a silver foil packet and ripped it open as he crawled onto the bed between my legs. Pulling the condom from the wrapper, I watched him quickly roll it over his shaft. Once done, he grabbed both my hands and pulled me up in a sitting position. Slowly, he slipped my open shirt off of my shoulders, tossing it to the floor. The bra came quickly after. "Better?"

I nodded. "Much."

"Good." Placing a hand on my chest, he slowly moved it upwards until his large, strong hand was poised over my throat. As he grasped my throat possessively, his lips crashed down onto mine with a passion that left me breathless.

We toppled back onto the bed together, his dick sliding between my legs. The feel of him so close to my entrance nearly drove me insane. My pussy was already so wet and lubricated that one slip and he'd be deep within me. I needed to feel him in me, spreading me. I needed him to bring me to heights he'd taken me to nearly a decade ago.

Releasing my throat, he slowly sat back, allowing his fingers to trail their way down my body. The closer his fingers got to my core the more I squirmed in anticipation. But when his fingers reached my mound, he didn't pause, instead moving upwards down my legs until he was sitting back fully on his heels. Grabbing my ankles in each hand, he slipped them over his shoulders, hoisting my ass up in the air. He leaned forward, his dick pressing at the entrance of my core.

"Tell me you want it. I want to hear it."

"I want you. I want you fucking me, Carrington," I gasped, clutching at the blanket under me as I tried to control the tremors rocking my body.

A smile spread across his lips and he nodded. "Your wish, ma'am." With one forceful thrust, he slammed into my drenched core, filling me to the max with his shaft.

I screamed out, my hands turning into fist around the handfuls of blankets beneath me.

Slowly he pulled out of me, leaving just the head remaining at my entrance.

"Carrington," I pleaded.

"You feel so fucking incredible," he groaned, slamming into me again. "So tight, and so ready."

"Yes!" The word hissed from me through clenched teeth.

"All mine."

He pulled out and pressed into me again and again, bringing me closer and closer to the summit. As he continued to pummel me, he slowly lowered himself, his hand grasping my throat again, pinning me to the mattress with just a slight pressure while his free hand planted itself on the side of my head doubling me over like a pretzel.

Suddenly his thrusts stopped being slow and sensual, taking on a fast and frenzied motion, his dick slamming into me further than I've ever had a man reach, stroking my G-spot with each thrust.

I was close. So close. The waves of pleasure crashing over me became so intense, I could barely breathe. I couldn't speak. All I could do was feel and pray for sweet release.

"Come for me again, baby. I need to feel it," he growled into my ear, the warmth of his breath sending a shimmy through me.

It was the sound of his voice sounding so raspy and feral that sent me spiraling into oblivion. My core tightened around him, holding him momentarily before I screamed out one more time as the dam broke. Tears formed at the corners of my eyes as relief more intense than I've ever felt before washed over me.

"Oh fuck!" Carrington grunted, slamming into me one final time and remaining there as his dick unloaded his seed. The tension within him seemed to immediately fade and he released my throat, instead running hasty kisses up my neck from my collarbone up to my chin and then ultimately to my lips.

When he released my legs, I slipped my arms around his neck and held onto him, pressing his hard, sweaty body against me. I couldn't remember feeling so fulfilled as I had right then. I wouldn't allow any thoughts of my past with this man to change things between us. I'd just allow myself to enjoy the night. The ramifications of what we'd just done was a problem for tomorrow.

Chapter 7

Carrington

Slowly waking up, it took me a moment to recall the events of the previous night. Part of me still had a hard time believing it had happened, but the weight holding my right arm down proved to me that it was true. Felicity slept silently next to me, cuddled up to my side. I felt a warm feeling creep up within me seeing her next to me. She'd been so hot and cold since I'd moved in and to see her so free, finally letting me in, was an amazing feeling. I felt like she'd finally allowed herself to open up to me for the first time since we met.

But I still had a nagging feeling that we knew each other and that she was keeping things from me. It was crazy, because I'd have recognized her if we'd met before, but being with her felt so familiar. It was a good feeling. Maybe we'd been soulmates in a different life? It wasn't like I really believed in that nonsense, but it was kind of a nice sentiment all the same.

Taking care not to disturb her, I reached over to the nightside table and grabbed my phone. Turning it on, I looked at the time and grimaced. It was later than I'd expected it to be, I had less than an hour to get to work. I had my first official by request appointment at 9am sharp, the last thing I wanted was to let them down – the shop or the client.

She was cuddled up tight to my side and looked so peaceful, it'd be a crime to wake her. Slowly, I began to inch my way out from under her, pausing at any little indication that I might wake her. It took close to ten minutes, but eventually, I managed to get out from under her grasp and slide off the bed.

Standing naked at the side of the bed, I raised my hands up and over my head giving my body a full stretch. The feel of the muscles being pulled felt incredible. I'd hit the gym after work. There was a small one in the basement of the building that had some basic equipment which would do.

Leaving the bedroom, I gave Misty a pat on the head as I entered the bathroom and took a quick shower. When working so closely to someone else, I certainly didn't need to be going to work smelling like sex. Once I was clean and fresh again, I toweled off, making my way back into the bedroom.

Upon entering the room, I paused in the doorway and looked at her for a moment. She had turned to her side, hugging the thick white comforter with one leg wrapped around it. Moving to my dresser, I grimaced when I heard it creak. Damned IKEA dresser. Removing a pair of jeans, t-shirt and underwear, I quickly got dressed and left the bedroom, closing the door behind me.

Misty greeted me, blocking my path to the door. Felicity was always up before me in the morning and would take the dog out, but by the way she looked up at me whimpering, I suspected a bathroom break was long past due. After last night, there was no telling when Felicity would get up.

Looking at my phone again, I groaned. I was seriously running low on time, but what could I do? I couldn't leave her to hold it or piss on the floor. Grabbing her leash, she did a little dance as I hooked it to her collar. "I swear if you have a massive shit for me to clean, your momma is going to owe me," I grumbled, leaving the apartment, rushing her downstairs and out the back of the building.

There was a small tuft of grass in the back of the building next to the dumpster where she was taken when we were short on time, which is where I led her and waited impatiently as she sniffed every damned blade of grass.

"I think you missed a patch of grass over there, Misty." Rolling my eyes, I turned to give her some privacy as she finally did her business. My nose curled up as I caught a whiff of a wretched stench. Hearing movement behind me, I turned to see the present she'd left me making me wonder if she'd crapped it out or a damned horse had instead.

"You've gotta be kidding me." Her little stub of a tail wagged furiously as I pulled a doggie doo bag from the dispenser clipped to the leash and proceeded to grab the monstrous turd, tie the bag and chuck it into the nearby garbage bin. "We need to get

you on a raw food diet or something old girl because that much shit can't be normal."
Her only answer was a nudge of her head into my hand demanding to be petted.

Taking her back into the apartment, I washed my hands thoroughly with scalding water before finally taking off to work.

~*~   TT   ~*~

Felicity

Why is my bed so hard? I yawned loudly as I arched my back and did a cat-like stretch on the way to the stiff bed. My head felt like it'd explode. Why did I have to drink so much?

Rubbing the sleep from my eyes, I slowly sat up and lowered my hands, looking around me. The contents in the room were not mine. My entire body froze in panic as the events of the previous night came rushing back to me in explicit detail.

"Oh no, no, no…" Flipping the comforter off me, I leapt from the bed in a frantic search for my clothing scattered all over.

I looked at the open door and into the kitchen. It didn't appear he was still home. Slowly, I crept towards the doorway gathering clothing as I went, attempting to hear any sound that would indicate if I was alone or not. Thankfully the only sounds to be heard was that of Misty loudly snoring on her bed next to the sofa.

Peeking from the room, a preliminary scan of the living areas confirmed I was indeed alone in the apartment. Rushing from the bedroom with my clothes bundled in my arms, I headed for my own room.

This was bad. It was so incredibly bad. It's not like we could just turn back time and forget it happened. It's also not like we could just not call or see each other. We lived together for fuck's sakes, so avoiding each other wasn't a possibility. How in the name of God could I have been so stupid was beyond me?

It was those damned vodka coolers. Why did I have to drink last night?

Snatching my phone from the table which still had the remains of our dinner on it, I looked at the time. It was already past noon! When he left and when he planned on getting back was beyond me, but I knew one thing, I needed to clean myself up and get this mess sorted out.

Maybe if I cleaned up all evidence of our night together, we could pretend it hadn't happened. We'd simply forget and move on with our lives as though nothing ever happened.

Entering my bedroom, I dumped the armful of clothing from my hands and into the clothes hamper. Step one complete.

Looking back out into the living room at Misty, I considered taking her out, but guessed Carrington had already done it otherwise Misty would have been full out whine mode by now. It was good of him to consider her; I'd give him kudos for that.

There's also something else I'd give him kudos for – the incredible way he'd made me feel last night. There were some parts that were a little hazy in my mind, but the vast majority were very clear and very vivid – like the way his tongue felt between my legs.

Dear God, that man knew how to use his tongue! Not to even get into how impressive his endurance was. My entire body shuddered as I remembered the jolts of electricity that'd raced down my spine each time the head of his dick pressed against my G-spot.

I shook my head. It wasn't the time to take a trip down memory lane. For all I knew, he was at work trying to forget the entire night. Or desperately seeking out a new place to live. The worst part of waking up alone after being with someone for the first time is not being able to access what they're thinking or feeling the next day.

After grabbing a quick shower, getting dressed and spending the next hour cleaning like a madwoman, I was finally able to sit back and relax on the sofa, satisfied I'd removed all evidence that Carrington and I had slept together. I was still attempting to figure out how I'd handle this situation when he eventually arrived home.

My phone buzzed and I picked it up, looking down at the screen at the incoming message. A part of me was disappointed upon discovering that it wasn't from Carrington. Instead, it was my mother asking me to call her immediately. Her urgent texts were never actually urgent, but if I didn't reply within the first ten minutes of her texting me, she'd start calling until I answered. She was worse than a stalker at times.

Dialing her number, I sighed trying to guess ahead of time what the urgent matter could be. It could be any number of things, from the caller at the bingo hall she liked frequently fumbling the numbers of the balls to the neighbor revving his sports car too loudly in the morning that in turn disturbed her morning coffee. Mom had a tendency of encompassing the stereotype of a "Karen" to a tee.

She answered on the first ring.

Mom: Hello?

Felicity*:* Hey Mom, what's up? You said it was urgent?

Mom: Yes! I've got some news tidbits for you.

I sighed and rolled my eyes. By news tidbits, she meant gossip.

Felicity: You don't say?

My mother laughed; I practically felt her excitement through the phone lines.

Mom: Yes! You won't believe it.

Felicity*:* Bet I can and will.

Mom: Well, guess who I ran into at the market this morning.

I laughed, shaking my head. I really didn't care, but her excitement was infectious.

Felicity*: Ryan Reynolds?*

Mom: No.

Felicity: Bill Gates?

Mom, starting to sound a little annoyed: Come on now, be serious dear. I haven't seen this person in years.

Felicity: Then I give up. Who'd you run into?

I swear, if I ever get to the point where I get this excited about running into some random person in the market, I hope someone shoots me in the fucking head.

Mom: Janet Anderson.

I remained silent for a moment as the name registered for me. Carrington's mom. What a coincidence. The morning after her son and I shagged, my mother runs into his mom.

Mom: Did you hear me?

Felicity: Yes, Mom. Why is that so urgent for me to know?

Mom*:* Well, as it turns out Carrington, the boy you went out with when you were kids, remember him? He lived not too far from us.

I snorted.

Felicity: Yeah, I think I may recall who he is.

Mom: Whatever happened between you two anyhow? He was such a handsome and polite young man.

Felicity: I don't remember, Mom. Please just get to the point.

Don't get me wrong, I loved my mother dearly, but the buildup in suspense with everything she said was tedious as best.

Mom: Carrington has moved to New York, Manhattan from what I hear! Isn't that crazy? You both live in Manhattan now!

Felicity: It's as though the entire situation was the creation of witches, Mom. You do realize that there are close to two million people living just in Manhattan. New York is the city many artists migrate to. It's not that hard to believe.

Mom: How'd you know that he was an artist?

Felicity: It was a random guess. He always liked to draw when we were younger.

Mom*:* You should look him up. Maybe you two can hook up.

I nearly laughed out loud. Too late for that. We'd hooked up extremely well last night already. I was tempted to tell my mother that Carrington and I had already met and he was my new roommate, but she was such a gossip, the chances of her keeping it to herself and not using it as a conversation starter with his mother was slim to none.

Felicity: I'll think about it. We never really got along in high school. It's not like we had a strong friendship, doubt he'd even remember who I was.

Mom: Oh sweetie, you don't give yourself enough credit.

Felicity: Thank you, Mom.

Mom: Have you found a new roommate yet?

Felicity: Not yet. I'll let you know when I do.

There was a light beeping sound coming from the other end of the phone.

Mom: Oh shoot. The bread I'm making is ready. I'll have to call you back.

Without waiting for a reply from me, she disconnected the call.

Chapter 8

Carrington

Our shop was an open concept shop with each of us having our own chair and work area, with everyone in full view of everyone else. Having it open concept seemed to make the place look larger and less intimidating.

The owner was the former winner of one of those reality TV tattooing competitions. She kept the place well-lit and always played upbeat music. Mostly top 40 stuff. And the décor was all whites, chrome and bright colors. It was definitely a nice place. I considered myself fortunate that they liked my work enough to invite me to apprentice here and learn from them.

We were in hour four of what I'd predicted to be a six-hour tattoo. My client, a man I assumed to be close to my age, had been quiet for most of the session keeping himself occupied with whatever movie he was watching on his phone. That was fine by me, I had a lot to go through in my head right now. Namely, how I'd deal with Felicity now that we'd had sex.

"You seem to be concentrating pretty hard there."

My head perked up from the tattoo and I shrugged. "Just making sure it's done well, that's all."

"I would've guessed you're having chick issues."

Laughing, I sat upright and groaned softly. I'd been crouched over for so long that my back was stiff and there was a dull ache across the lower part. "I don't know if I'd say issues exactly."

My client grabbed his bottle of water and took a long drink. "Let me guess, you're not really a one chick, settling down kinda guy. But you've found a girl that you like. So now you're conflicted because you don't want to lose that wild stallion sort of life, but you really like her." He cocked a brow at me. "Am I even a little close to the truth here?"

Chuckling, I placed the tattoo gun on the tray and pulled off the black latex gloves from my hands, then sat back in the chair. I needed a break anyhow. We'd been going for way too long without taking one. "Maybe. That apparent? You've been there?"

"It is and I have." He lifted his left arm, the opposite arm than the one I'd worked on, showing me the wedding band on his finger. "I had no desire to get hitched or settle down. I'm only thirty-one, but sometimes what you think you want and what you end up wanting are two entirely different things."

"You don't say."

"Yeah. I never wanted a relationship. Hit it and quit it. Keep the girl's number on my phone with a note attached on how they ranked in the sack so I knew who to call first if I wanted to get laid."

Rubbing my chin, I laughed again. "Well, I don't have them ranked or anything, but my favorites are starred. I haven't been here for very long – like six months – so the list isn't overly extensive yet."

"And you've already found someone who's done more than catch your interest." He said it as a statement of fact, not a question.

"Well, it's complicated."

"It always is, buddy. Always is. What's the problem?" Grabbing a bag of chips from the table next to him, he cracked open the bag and began eating them. "Snack break, you don't mind?"

"Not at all."

"I'll be your love guru while we take a break. So, tell me the problem. What's wrong with the girl?"

Sighing, I thought about Felicity. She was hot and cold a lot, but that wasn't a big deal. It was a matter of reading her mood and I'd gotten better at it. "There's nothing wrong with her. She's beautiful, talented, and independent. She's an amazing woman."

"Okay, so then what's the problem? Are you thinking you can do better?"

"No, it's not that. She's my roommate and so even if I were interested in something more than a one-night thing with her, if things went south then I'd be fucked. You know how hard it is to get a decent place and good roommate in this city, it's like winning the lottery. I don't want to mess that up."

"Is that really why?"

"Partially yes."

"How many relationships have you been in?"

Laughing, I shrugged. "I'm not really into that."

"Man, we're not getting any younger and trust me when I say once you hit thirty, it's no longer fun to be single and jumping from bed to bed. It just gets lonely and depressing."

"Boy, you're a ray of sunshine." Grabbing a new pair of gloves from the dispenser, I pulled them on.

"Just keeping it real my man. I've got a wife now and a baby on the way and it beats the fuck out of being single and having one-night stands. Trust me. Once you find a woman who really understands you and you feel is special in every way, you need to snatch her up before someone else comes along and grabs her while you're still making up your mind."

My client placed the halfway-eaten bag of chips on the rack and settled into the seat. "From one retired player to another. You should think about what I said." Without waiting for my reply, he placed his headphones back over his ears and restarted the movie, leaving me with my own thoughts.

I'd never really given my ways much thought. Up until now, it just worked. I'd never really wanted the responsibility of having someone depend on me, I supposed. Hadn't really thought about why I wouldn't commit. It just never appealed to me.

Though, he was right. I was in my late twenties now and wasn't getting any younger. Maybe it was time to really give a thought to where my life was headed. I knew I always wanted a wife and kid one day; it'd just never been a priority.

Picking up the gun, I dipped it in the ink and got back to work. Maybe by the time I was done with his piece, I'd have been able to sort through some answers that'd failed to come to me at the moment.

The last couple of hours of the piece flew by and I couldn't say that I was any closer to figuring out how I felt than I was when I first stepped into the shop this morning. If anything, I was even more confused because now I'd rethought my entire way of doing things in my personal life.

Shading the final part of the tattoo, I turned off the machine, placed the gun on the tray and peeled off my gloves as I sank back into the seat, admiring my work. I'd only been tattooing a short while, but I was pleased with the realistic lioness I'd created on his arm. I bordered the lioness with a ring of leaves with the name Caitlyn at the bottom. It wasn't the quality that my boss could achieve, but I was happy with the result.

"It's all done." Tossing the gloves in the trash can, I waited to hear my client's verdict.

Getting up from the chair, he groaned and gave his torso a couple of twists. "I'm telling ya man. You hit thirty and shit just starts hurting." My client looked at his new art on his arm from every angle possible in the full-length mirror of my work area. "Dude, this is fucking incredible. The wife is going to bawl her eyes out. She's insanely sentimental."

Getting up from the chair, I came to stand behind him, admiring the piece in the mirror, pleased he was happy. Maybe my work today scored me a regular client. Maybe he'd tell a friend or two. That'd be amazing. "I'm glad you're happy with it."

~*~ TT ~*~

Felicity

He hadn't texted or called all morning or afternoon. It made me feel anxious. Mostly because I didn't know how I felt about us myself. I had a sinking suspicion that he'd pretend last night never happened.

Could I do the same? Though it's not like I had a choice. Better question yet was did I want it to go anywhere or should I just chalk it up to a drunken' night of stress relief?

Sitting on the window ledge, I looked down at my computer screen. The words of a client of mine flashed in front of my eyes, but I wasn't registering the words. I'd tried to edit the first chapter of her book three times now; I'd never make the deadline I promised to have it back to her by at this rate. Realistically, I knew the issue. I wouldn't be able to get anything accomplished until Carrington got home and I felt him out and found out where he stood with us.

Skipping back to the start of the novel, I'd just began to edit it for the fourth time when I heard the key being inserted in the lock.

Just play it cool. You don't even know what you want from him yet. Hell, you have one big fat lie hanging over your head as it was anyhow. Even if he wanted to pursue something with you, did you want to start a relationship with a lie? A voice in the back of my head reasoned. It was right.

I pretended to be hard at work when the door swung open and Carrington stepped inside with a couple brown paper bags of groceries in his arms.

Looking up, I gave him a hesitant smile. "Hey."

"Hey." He returned my smile. "I stopped by the market and grabbed some things. Figured if you haven't had dinner yet then maybe you'd be interested in me making us some burgers and fries." Placing the bags on the countertop, he pulled a pack of ground beef from one of the bags and held it up for me to see.

"Great, I've been working since I got up and haven't had a chance to eat yet." At the mention of food, my stomach grumbled.

"I can hear it over here. You know the kitchen isn't all that far, you can take a break from time to time and get something to eat."

"Yeah, I know this, but I'm just into getting this done." Looking down at the page, the big, bold "Chapter One" header mocked me.

"All work and no play."

"Do you need help?" I started to set my laptop aside, but he waved me off.

"No, I'm fine. I prefer to cook on my own. I've always been particular about that."

I nodded, chewing at my lower lip wondering if I should mention the previous evening or not.

Once he had everything put away and the burgers into the frying pan, he looked at me across the room with a frown on his face. "Listen, I was hoping to talk to you about something. About last night." His voice was solemn, matching his expression.

My heart sank.

I hadn't known what I wanted to do in regard to us, but by the look on his face I had a feeling I wasn't going to have a say either way. Deciding to beat him to the punch to save at least a little face, I shrugged. "It's not a big deal. There was some tension, we had sex. Not a biggie. We just go back to how things were and pretend it didn't happen."

As the words left my lips, I knew I was lying. Partially drunk or not, it kinda was a big deal for me, but what could I do? He didn't want me back when we were kids and that hadn't changed even though I'd reinvented myself.

Chapter 9

Carrington

I paused for a moment, letting her words sink in. "Yeah." Running a hand through my hair, I nodded my head. "That's what I was thinking. I'm glad we're on the same page."

She nodded and went back to work.

I can't say I knew what to expect from her when I came home, but I was pretty sure she'd dumped my ass before we even had a chance to explore if we were good together. I hadn't really had a gameplan when I'd arrived. My intent was to discuss what her feelings were over supper and then go from there. I guess she made that pretty easy. Brutal but easy.

When it came right down to it, I should've been relieved she didn't want to make it weird. Whenever that happened with any other girl, I'd have given a big sigh of relief. It didn't feel like much of a relief this time though.

As I flipped the burgers and checked on the french fries, I mulled over what had just happened. We'd go back to being pals. I could start dating and life would go on.

My phone buzzed on the counter behind me. Turning, I picked it up and looked down at the screen surprised to see it was Sophia, the motel owner's daughter.

Sophia: How is your new place?

I looked across the room at Felicity and smiled, despite the uncertainty that was messing with my head at the moment.

Carrington: It's pretty good. Nice to be out of the motel room and be able to wash my clothes. ⍰

Sophia: LOL. We got the washer and dryer replaced. They work now.

Carrington: Had to wait until I left. You figured my clothes would stink too bad to clean in a brand new washer?

Sophia: LMAO. You're so silly. It's just a coincidence.

Turning back to the stove, I flipped the fries and turned the heat off on the burgers while starting to brown the buns.

Sophia: I miss having you here.

Carrington: Do you miss me or the sex?

Sophia: Maybe a little bit of both. We had a good time.

Carrington: We did. I appreciate everything you did for me. You and your dad.

Sophia: My father decided that he didn't want to get a tattoo after all, he just can't think of something he really wants. So I convinced him to let me take his place. Would you mind inking a virgin instead of Dad?

Carrington: I have no problem with that. Virgin skin is my favorite. You never forget your first.

Sophia: That's how I'm thinking about it. Would you mind swinging by the motel and doing it here? You forgot a hoodie here anyhow so I figured you might want it.

Carrington: Sure, next week? Sound good? I'll take the day off work and drop by.

Smoke started to rise from inside of the oven. Shit!

Carrington: Gotta run. Chat later.

Not waiting for a reply, I tossed the phone onto the counter and attended to the fries. They looked all right except for a few of the really small ones that were more like little dark chunks of charcoal than french fries at this point.

It had been fun with Sophia. She was a wonderful and incredibly sexy girl. But something was lacking. I hadn't felt that connection with her, not like I'd with Felicity.

Yet here you are being tossed into the friendzone, a voice at the back of my mind scoffed at me.

Ignoring the voice, I plated the burger and fries and took them to the table. "Supper is served."

Felicity looked up and smiled, setting her laptop to the side and coming over to the table taking the chair she normally sat in. "You didn't need to do this, but thank you. It smells delicious."

I hesitated looking down at her as memories flooded me of dropping to my knees and devouring her pussy last night. Clearing my throat, I shook my head, freeing the memories from my mind as I sat across from her.

Normally silence between us was comfortable, but tonight there was a tension so thick, you could cut it with a knife. I didn't like it at all. It was a mix of sexual energy and unsaid thoughts and feelings that neither one of us wanted to bring up.

She was the one that broke the silence. "How was your first non-walkin-in hand-me-down client?"

"It was good. I think it turned out well." Picking up my phone that was placed face down next to me, I opened my gallery and brought up the picture of the lioness tattoo and then slid the phone across the table to her.

Picking up the phone, she brought it to eye level and examined the tattoo. Eventually she nodded a soft smile spreading across her lips. "That's good. I mean really good work. I can't believe you've only been tattooing a few weeks now. You're really a natural."

A sense of pride welled up within me. I'd worked hard to learn the technique of tattooing and develop my talents doing everything from sitting in and getting pointers from the boss to watching the tattooing competitions and studying all the different styles. There were many more than I'd originally thought. Lots to master from the traditional, to portraits, to morphs and everything in between.

"I'm still trying to figure out my style and what I like to tattoo the best. I'm leaning towards realism, but I'm just too new at it to make a decision either way."

She nodded. "I love it."

"Yeah the guy had gotten it for his anniversary. His wife loves lions and he said that she was his lioness."

"Aww." She smiled warmly. "Caitlynn is his wife then?"

"It is. He's hoping she'll love it."

"I know if a man made that type of commitment to me then I'd be overwhelmed. Sure if things went south, then it can be removed or covered up, but you have to really be committed to someone to brand your body with them even if it's an image that only the two of you would know is meaningful."

"I had a good chat with him."

"That so?" She looked up from my phone to meet my gaze.

"Yeah, he mentioned he wasn't much for commitment until he met her. He said he knew almost immediately that she was special and she was the one he was meant to be with."

"That's sweet. I hope to one day find that." She paused, looking deep into my eyes. "That we both find that."

Taking a deep breath in, I smiled at her. "Maybe that's not all that far away. Maybe it's right before your eyes, you just don't know it yet."

Our gazes locked and the tension slowly evaporated. Maybe the conversation we'd had when I got home was a misunderstanding. Misunderstandings and unsaid thoughts seemed to be our thing.

"Listen, Felicity…" I began to reach across the table to take her free hand, but the buzzing of my phone interrupted the moment.

She began to hand it over then hesitated when her eyes shifted down. I saw her reading the message that had come in. A feeling of dread washed over me. The smile faded from her beautiful lips and they turned into a hard line, her forehead creased.

Fuck. Whatever came in couldn't be good.

Quickly, she recovered and placed the phone face down in front of me at the table. "If you don't mind, I'm just going to take this to my room. I have some work to do and I really think I need to get to it. I've got a deadline and all."

She didn't wait for my reply. Standing, she took her plate and made her way to the bedroom, stopping just long enough to grab her laptop from the ledge. Entering her room, she slammed the door behind her with a definitive thump that actually shook the casing around it.

Fuck my life.

I looked down at the phone for a moment dreading what the message that set her off could possibly be. Picking it up I looked down at the message.

Sophia: Just the thought of you coming over makes me wet. Can't wait to have you take my virginity. ▯

Dropping the phone onto the table with disgust, I dropped my head into my hands and groaned. Of course, Sophia would text when the phone was in Felicity's hands. Could I ever catch a damn break?

Picking my head up, I looked at the closed bedroom door as I leaned back into the chair. I had no fucking clue what to do at this point. I wasn't one to believe in fate or destiny, but maybe it was a sign that I wasn't ready for a commitment with anyone. Perhaps it was the universe's way of stopping something that may hurt Felicity before it even began.

Perhaps this was just for the best. She was my roommate and mixing business with pleasure was never a good idea. This was no exception.

Looking down at the phone I re-read Sophia's message. My dick didn't jerk alive at the thought of her like it normally would've.

"Fuck it," I muttered to the empty room. This was why I never got involved with women before fucking. They just brought too much aggravation and drama for my life.

Carrington: Looking forward to seeing you again. I'll get back to you later with a date and time.

Chapter 10

Felicity

Entering the café, I spotted my friend and editing client, Alicia, at a little bistro table towards the back. I'd worked with her for several years and she was one of the few friendships I had in the city. Noticing me, she smiled and waved.

Stopping at the counter, I placed my order with the barista and once my frappuccino was prepared and served, I made my way over to Alicia. Taking a sip from the frappuccino I moaned, the chocolate-coffee flavor was to die for.

"You look amazing," I said, sitting down across from her. And she did. Her dark curly hair reached her shoulders and was always perfectly in place and she had the most intense brown – nearly black eyes with the most perfect chocolate brown skin.

"You look stunning as usual."

"Thank you."

"So, tell me what's going on?" Leaning back against the metal hair she crossed her arms over her chest.

"What do you mean? It's all good." I shrugged, trying to be nonchalant, but failing miserably.

"Whenever you want to give me the comments on one of my books personally, it's usually because you want to talk about something that's bothering you. So spill it lady."

Grasping the back of my neck, I gave it a gentle squeeze attempting to relieve some of the tension building within. "Well, you know I was getting a new roommate. A man this time. Figured it would work out better."

She nodded. "I'm aware. You mentioned it the last time we spoke. How'd it go? Is he eating all your food? Does he have chronic flatulence and stinking up the place? I told you boys are gross to live with."

Laughing, I shook my head. "No, it's nothing like that. He buys his own food. Even cooks me dinner from time to time. And he smells amazing. Fresh, like when he's had a swim in the ocean and as he's walking in from the water a gust of wind hits his back sending a light, sea breeze of pure man to your nose."

She threw her head back and laughed, a light pleasant sound. She easily had one of the loveliest laughs I'd ever heard. "That's descriptive, maybe I should have you writing my books for me. I'll need to steal that sometime."

"By all means."

"So what's the problem then?"

Digging my phone from inside my white leather purse, I brought up my photo gallery and started searching until I found a picture of myself back in high school, then passed it to her.

Giving me a dubious look, she glanced down at the photo and frowned. "I'm not following."

"Does that person look familiar?"

She looked up from the phone to meet my gaze. "Should it?"

"That's me. Back in high school." I was embarrassed to show that picture, but I needed her to understand my reasoning. "I used my first name Connie back then. I've been going by my middle name Felicity since high school."

Looking back down at the picture, her mouth fell open. "Wow. I'd never know. Not in a million years. You're the exact opposite to the person in that picture. Literally nothing is the same."

"Exactly why there's a problem. The summer before high school started, I dated my new roommate for a little while. Then he dumped me when high school started. He didn't want to be associated with the ugly, fat nerd."

"You obviously don't like this guy, so why in the hell did you let him move in with you?"

I shrugged. "I don't know. He was the best I'd met and he really needed a place. It was an impulsive decision. I figured I could just let it go and not really spend much time with him. Kinda hoped he'd changed. I don't know."

"Does he know who you are?"

"Nope. No clue. But that's only part of the problem." Frowning, I continued the words coming out of me rapidly like a bout of verbal diarrhea. "I like him, but he's the same player he was back in high school. We got tipsy and had sex a few nights ago, it just felt right. The next day, he came home and just when it seemed like we were having a moment, some girl texted him excited about him coming over to fuck her. Literally the night after we'd had sex he was planning on screwing some other chick. I was willing to drop my shields and thought we had something. Or at least we could've had something."

I sniffed, surprising myself. At that moment, I realized how strongly I'd felt for him. But it didn't matter though. It's not like we'd end up a couple.

"You're not going to tear up over a man." Grabbing a napkin from the dispenser, she leaned forward and passed it to me.

"I know, this is twice in a lifetime that I've been in tears over him. You have to keep in mind one important thing."

"Which is? Until the night you two had sex, he had no idea what you felt for him. You said yourself that the sex was alcohol induced. Maybe he'd planned that little sexfest with that girl before you two had your night together. If you gave him the cold shoulder then perhaps he figured you regretted it? There's so many variables. You know what would fix the confusion?"

I shrugged.

"Talk to him." She passed me the phone back, the picture of my sad and pathetic teenaged self still staring at me. "And maybe let him in on the fact that you two had a past together."

"I don't want to be that girl anymore, Alicia."

"But you still *are* that girl. You may not look like her anymore, but you're still her. What if you two make up? And what if he discovers he knew you back in the day, don't you think he's going to get pissed because you lied to him? Yes, you haven't actually lied, but omitting a huge part of who you are is just like lying."

I groaned, tossing the phone into my handbag. "I know. I've been avoiding it. My mother even called me the other day telling me she ran into his mother. She thought it might be fun if we reconnected."

Alicia laughed. "Well mission accomplished on that front."

"So just tell him, huh?"

"That's what I'd do… You know, if I were interested in a relationship with someone – which I'm not."

"Yeah, I think I recall you mentioning that from time to time," I teased, my laughter subsiding and I grew serious again. "Listen, thank you for your help. I think you're right. I think I need to sit down and have a chat with him. I just have to gather the balls to do it."

Alicia winked at me. "I know you can do it. You didn't spend all the time and effort that you did to reinvent yourself just to chicken out on telling someone you've got the feels for that you're into them. What's the worst that can happen? Him telling you he's not into you? If he's not because of who you both were back in high school, then you definitely don't need him in your life."

Spreading my hands out at my side, I nodded. "When you're right, you're right."

Smiling, she leaned forward. "Now tell me, how in love with my new novel are ya?"

~*~ TT ~*~

Leaving the coffee shop, I grabbed my phone from my purse and pulled up Carrington's number. Like a Band-Aid right off.

Felicity: Hey Carrington, are you still at work? Can we talk?

As I waited for him to respond, I began to walk my way towards the tattoo shop where he worked. Maybe I could bring him a sandwich as a way to break the ice? There was a deli not far from his work that he loved to eat at.

A half hour later, I entered the deli. As if he'd sensed my closeness, my phone buzzed.

Carrington: I'm just finishing up with a client. What's up?

Felicity: I'm at the deli you like. I can grab you a sandwich and we could meet at the park down the street. Turkey and bacon club sound enticing?

Carrington: Sure does. ⍰ Meet you there in ten minutes?

Felicity: It's a date.

The line wasn't all that long, so I was in and out in less than five minutes.

Carrington was already at the park by the time I arrived.

He looked up as I approached and smiled. "Hey you, I'm glad you came over. I was hoping we could talk. I just wasn't sure how to go about it."

Passing him the sandwich wrapped in brown paper, I sat down next to him. "Not sure I like the way you're starting with this."

"Why?" Accepting the sandwich, he opened it up with a smile spreading across his lips as he looked down at his lunch and he immediately lost his train of thought. "This looks amazing. I haven't eaten all day. I had a last minute walk-in. Wanted a large leg piece of all things. Crazy. Had to design the thing on the spot and ink it."

Opening my sandwich, also a turkey and bacon club, I took a bite. "That's wild..." I hesitated. "But to get back to what it was that you wanted to talk to me about..."

"Oh yes." He put the sandwich, which was now nearly halfway done, back onto the wrapping. "I've noticed that it's been a little awkward between us since..."

I popped a shoulder as I inhaled sharply. "Our night together."

"I know. I haven't been sure how to fix it. And I know you saw that message from Sophia. I wasn't sure how to explain it or even if you'd be interested in talking to me. Was hoping you'd come to talk to me when you were ready."

"And what if I didn't?"

"Then I'd have eventually figured out a way to approach you when I knew you'd calmed down. You've pretty much kept yourself locked in your room the past few days, so assumed you weren't ready."

"Did you go visit your *friend* that texted you?" The word friend came out of my mouth dripping with sarcasm.

"No, not yet. If you'd read the entire conversation you'd have seen that she wants a tattoo. She's the daughter of the motel owner. The motel I was living at for a bit before moving in with you, you know the one. I'd traded the room in exchange for a tattoo when he wanted one. He told Sophia she could take his spot, so she just wanted me to come by to get it done."

"Sounded a little more intimate than that." My eyes narrowed at him. "Have you slept with her before?"

He shifted on the bench. When he looked back up at me, I didn't need him to verbally confirm my suspicions. I already knew. "Look, I knew her before I met you and I legit wasn't planning on a hook-up. I wasn't even sure where you and I stood. I had no idea what you thought after we slept together. You avoided me, and just when we were breaking ground, that stupid text fucked it all up."

"You've said on countless occasions you're not really a commitment guy. And you're not really into the monogamous thing."

"You never gave me a chance to even consider something different. You never gave me a chance, Felicity."

"Are you saying you're reconsidering your interest in monogamy?"

The charming smile that made my heart do a little flip-flop spread across his lips. "Never said I wasn't open to change."

I cocked a brow at him. "In that case, what do we do now? We're roommates, this could get complicated."

"It's already complicated, baby." Hooking his index finger under my chin, he lifted my face so I looked up into his stunning blue eyes. Lowering his head, he grazed his lips across mine so lightly I hardly believed it happened. "We're down the rabbit hole at this point." Pressing his forehead against mine, I closed my eyes and savored the feel of his closeness, our breaths intermingling.

"Carrington," I whispered, just as his lips captured mine with more force and passion. Moaning against his lips, he took the invitation to slip his tongue past my lips to frolic with mine. It felt so familiar – so good.

I was quickly on my way to losing myself in him when his phone buzzed, interrupting our moment. He groaned against my lips and reluctantly pulled away.

"Sorry." Giving me an apologetic smile, he pulled his phone from his back pocket and brought up his messages.

I almost expected to see that girl Sophie's name on the message, but it wasn't. The message was from Hailey.

"My boss," he explained.

"I know." Sitting back on the bench, I diverted my gaze not wanting to appear nosy.

"I've gotta go. Another walk-in client wants a job done and I'm the only artist available."

My heart sank a little. "I understand."

Wrapping up his sandwich he leaned into me and gave me another kiss. "Will you go on a date with me tonight, after work?"

"What do you have in mind?"

"Not sure yet. But I'll figure it out by the time I get home." He took a step away from me, turned and leaned in for another quick peck before jogging off in the direction of the shop.

With a wide grin on my face, I looked down at the sandwich feeling lighter in my heart than I'd felt in a long time. I'd tell him the truth about me later. There'd be lots of time on our date.

Chapter 11

Carrington

This was definitely a step for me. I'd never in my twenty-eight years had anything remotely resembling a relationship, yet here I was, a few hours from getting home and taking Felicity on an official date. Not a hangout. Not a coffee or a Netflix and chill, but a real date. It felt strange, I was actually a little scared along with excited. Maybe it was time for me to take life seriously. Did I really want to be in my thirties or even forties still chasing pussy, yet never having anything meaningful?

If I was completely honest with myself, that's not what I wanted, I'd been only telling myself that's what I wanted. The more I got to know Felicity, the more I saw life from a different angle. We were already living together so it's not like there would be any change, aside from sleeping in the same bed and being intimate.

"Looks like you've got something on your mind, brother," the man in my chair said.

Straightening in my chair, I looked up from his chest where I was tattooing the head of an elephant and looked into his eyes. The client was roughly my age and had been pretty quiet the entire session, until now.

"Yeah, I've got some things going on at home."

"Wifey giving ya trouble?"

I laughed. "Nah, it's complicated, but the jest of it is I have an important date with someone tonight. I gotta make sure it's perfect and I have no idea where to take her and funds are a little tight."

"This girl special to you?"

Smiling, I slowly nodded. "Yeah, I think so. Definitely has potential and I don't say that about just anyone." I huffed. "Never said that about anyone else before, to be honest."

"Hmm." He scratched at the scruff on his chin. "How about we work out a little trade?"

Placing the tattoo gun on the tray, I considered for a moment. "What kind of trade?"

"Well, I just happen to manage a dinner cruise. We do a nice tour of the Manhattan skyline, a little sail past the Statue of Liberty. The dinner is fine dining with an extensive menu, very romantic and we have a live band each night. It's fairly formal and extremely romantic. So you'll need to wear a suit – and a tie."

Laughing, I nodded. "Believe it or not, I *do* own a suit."

"Then you're golden. Now this is normally a pretty expensive cruise, but how about we trade the tattoo for the cruise for two?"

I mulled it over. I'd never done any of the tourist stuff in the city – not yet and I'd really wanted to do a cruise on the Hudson. Those things were stupidly expensive, and I just could never justify the cost of doing it. But Felicity would be that excuse and I couldn't think of anything else that'd show I was serious about having an exclusive relationship than with a gesture like that.

After a moment, I smiled and extended my hand to him. "If you can get us on that boat tonight, then you've got yourself a deal."

"Even though it's summer, it's still mid-week. There will be some vacancies, so I guarantee it can happen. Trust me, if you're looking to make this girl feel special, then this is the way to do it. Just give them my name when you arrive and I'll have a table waiting for you."

My lips curled into a smile, "I'd really appreciate that, brother."

~*~   TT   ~*~

Felicity

I looked down at the text Carrington had sent me, feeling butterflies flutter within my stomach. What did he have up his sleeve?

Carrington: I've got something extra special lined up for you. Make sure you're ready for a night you'll never forget.

It left me anxious, unsure of how to dress for this. Finally, I decided to text him back.

Felicity: Any clues on how I should dress for this?

Carrington: None. Maybe a sexy little dress. You know the saying, you can never go wrong with a little black dress.

Opening my small closet, I thumbed through the dresses hanging up. I really didn't have much to choose from. Maybe I should make a run to Macy's? After some back and forth in my head, I finally decided shopping would be the way to go. I rarely bought new clothes for myself, so I was long past due anyhow.

I was closing the closet when the apartment door opened. "Honey, I'm home," Carrington called out.

Fuck! So much for the shopping trip. Opening the closet back up, I grabbed two of the sexiest dresses I owned, spun and placed them flat onto the bed. "Awesome! It'd be really nice if you'd give me an idea of what to wear. I'm really stressed over this." Turning from the bed, I went to the bedroom doorway and peeked out.

Tossing his backpack onto the floor near the kitchen counter, Carrington caught my gaze. "You're free to go without clothing, but I'm not sure if we'd make it out the door if you do."

Rolling my eyes at him, I responded. "Or, you could give me an idea of what I should wear." Ducking back into the room, I grabbed the two dresses that I'd picked out and brought them into the living room, holding each of them up to myself.

The first one was a form-fitting short-sleeved, black dress with a skirt that flared out falling just above the knee. The second was a strapless little red dress that landed mid-thigh. It wasn't my favorite since it tended to be uncomfortable, but it did certainly qualify for sexy.

"Hmmm," he eyed both dresses with intense scrutiny. "I think that you may need to strip down and let me see them both on you so I can get a really good idea of how they'll look."

"I'm not doing that."

"Then I don't have enough information to be able to give you an educated answer."

"You're a putz."

"Ouch." He clutched at his chest and took a staggered step backwards. "Is this the kind of verbal abuse I can expect from you now that we're dating?"

With a huff, I shook my head, spun on my heel and entered my bedroom, closing the door behind me, ignoring the laughter from the other room. He was frustrating, but at the same time so fucking adorable. It was crazy how far we'd come in such a short time, despite our misunderstandings.

But he still needed to know the truth.

I'd tell him after our date.

Besides, it wasn't all that important. It had taken some time, but I'd gotten over what happened in the past. From time to time, it hit me like a tiny pin prick, but when it came down to it, the people we were in the past weren't who we were today. He was a reasonable guy, he'd see that as well. He wouldn't see Connie the Cow after I told him who I was back then. He'd see me, the woman he wants to have a relationship with.

He had to…

Deciding to pick comfort over sexy, I chose the black dress. It took me a while to apply my make-up, I kept obsessing over everything I applied. I'd never felt so nervous as I was for this date, which told me one thing – I was falling hard for him. Could I possibly be in love with him? Already? Despite everything?

No…

Once done, I did a quick inspection in the mirror and gave myself an approving nod. A part of me missed having long hair, but the pixie cut was just so easy to maintain. Maybe I'd grow it out?

Clearing my mind, I stood and made my way out of the bedroom and into the living room. As if sensing I was ready, the door on the opposite side of the room opened and out stepped Carrington.

My mouth dropped open and I was rendered speechless as I stared at him. He wore a black suit with the top button buttoned, complete with a blue tie that matched the hue of his eyes to perfection. He looked like a fucking movie star at a Hollywood premier.

He shifted uncomfortably from one foot to the other. "Either I look amazing or ridiculous. I only have one suit. Suits aren't really my thing. Does it look okay?" He flicked a piece of lint from the lapel of his suit, looking back at me with an insecurity I'd never seen in his eyes before. "Well, say something."

"You look… Just… Wow." Crossing the room, I slid my hands up his chest to entwine my fingers behind his neck. Pressing my body flush against his, I reached up, urging his head down for a kiss.

"You look amazing yourself, baby," he whispered, brushing his lips across mine. "Just a forewarning, if we don't get out of here now, I won't be able to hold myself accountable for what happens next. That would suck since I have a pretty cool date planned for us."

Chapter 12

Carrington

"Where are we going?" she asked for the hundredth time.

"You're not very good with surprises, are you?" Exiting the subway station, I took her hand in mine and led her towards the docks. Her heels made light tik-tik-tik sounds along the pavement as she walked.

Her cheeks took on a rosy hue. "I'm the worst with surprises. Regardless of whether someone is surprising me or if I'm surprising the other person. It's next to impossible for me to keep a surprise for someone else to myself. I guarantee when your birthday comes up next month, you'll know what I got you way in advance even though the plan will be to keep it a secret."

"That a fact?" As I spoke, it made me wonder how she knew my birthday was coming up. I wasn't all that keen on people knowing when it was, so I kept my birthday to myself for the most part to avoid anyone making a fuss.

She grimaced. "It is."

"How did you know it was my birthday next month? Are you checking up on me, Miss Boyce?"

Her face blanched. "I -" Looking up, a wide grin spread across her lips. "Are we going on a boat trip?"

Inhaling sharply, I loudly blew the air back out in a huff. "Busted. Was hoping you wouldn't guess until we were on the ship. I forget how perceptive you can be."

Laughing, she elbowed me in the ribs. "Dufus. It's pretty hard to miss the big ship or the fact we're walking down the docks towards it."

"Maybe I thought you'd enjoy a cool night swim."

"Right. I've always wondered what it was like to swim while wearing a sundress. In all honesty, I'm not much of a swimmer."

"No? Why not? You can't or just don't like to?"

"Just don't like it. Guess I've always felt insecure in a swimsuit, so I've avoided the beach and pools."

Taking a step back from her, I gave her a hard look up and down. "Why in the hell would you feel insecure? You've got a figure most women would kill for."

She shrugged, giving me a rueful smile. "Wasn't always like that."

Strange thing to say. I was about to crack a joke, asking if it was because she used to be five-hundred pounds or something, but perhaps she'd been chubby in the past and it was a sensitive spot for her, so I held my tongue. In my experience, women had a tendency to be sensitive about their weight.

"I used to be on the swim team in high school. Was pretty good."

Felicity's blue eyes looked up at me and she smiled. "That doesn't surprise me in the least."

"No?"

"Nah, it's pretty obvious you're the athletic type."

Finding the boat we were booked to be on, I let out a low whistle. My client hadn't been kidding when he'd said it was a beautiful boat and a great experience. The yacht was amazing, several floors, screaming money. Everyone walking up the ramp and into the ship was dressed to impress with expensive suits and jewels.

"Wow… Carrington. I can't believe you booked this!" As we reached the gates, a man in a suit with an iPad in his hands looked up and requested to see our tickets. I lowered my voice, "This must cost a fortune."

Standing before the gentlemen with the iPad I said, "We don't have tickets. We were invited by Gary Hennessey. He said you'd check the list. It's under Carrington

Anderson." If we weren't on the list, I'd have to think of something pretty awesome quickly to save face.

He looked at the iPad screen and frowned. "I don't see anything here under that name."

Well, shit.

"Are you sure? Gary assured me we'd be on the list."

The guy at the gate shook his head. "I'm not seeing anything. I'm so sorry, sir."

So much for impressing Felicity. My mind swirled with potential ideas. Maybe I could find us a nice restaurant accepting walk-ins. Maybe we could get some scalped tickets for a Broadway play?

"Did I hear my name, Eric?"

I let out a sigh of relief when Gary appeared at the top of the ramp, making his way down to us. Looking up at us, he smiled. "Carrington! I'm glad you made it, I set aside a table special for you." Clapping the doorman on the shoulder, he continued, "This guy here is an amazing artist. The tat he gave me this afternoon was insane and at the last minute. If you want work done this is the man to see."

A sense of pride welled up in me. "Thank you. I'm just doing my job."

"Come. Follow me." He waved us forward. "The weather couldn't be more perfect. Though they're predicting there may be rain later tonight. Fingers crossed that doesn't happen."

"We've definitely gotten lucky." He was right, the weather couldn't have been more perfect than it was tonight. The skies were clear and while it was hot out, there was just enough breeze to cool you down. We made our way upstairs and true to his word, he had the best table in the place set aside for us, tucked nicely away in the back away from the other diners.

"I hope this will be to your liking," Gary asked.

"Are you kidding?!" Felicity exclaimed. "This is beyond. It's something you'd expect to see in a movie."

Gary laughed. "I appreciate that. We do our best to give our customers a premium experience." Grabbing the back of the chair furthest from us he pulled it out. "My lady."

She giggled as she released my hand and settled herself onto the chair, looking up at me with excitement in her eyes. It felt good to see her so happy and to know that I was the one to give her this experience. Maybe I'd been missing something by not taking relationships seriously.

"The server will be around with menus and a wine list shortly. If you have any issues or need anything, have your server give me a holler." With that, he disappeared, stopping periodically to greet some of the other guests along the way.

The middle-aged graying waiter approached us just as the ship jerked and began to move. Looking out the window, the dock slowly moved behind us. "Welcome to the ship. I have some menus for you both." The waiter handed us both a one-page menu and a two-page wine list.

Looking down at the menu, I internally cringed. The prices were insane. Quickly, I did a count in my head of the money in my bank account, deciding I wouldn't have a choice but to put it on my credit card.

"The captain wanted me to make sure that you enjoyed yourself and said to enjoy anything on the menu. I can recommend some wines if you like. It will all be on the house. The only thing you need to worry about is having a good time tonight."

I sighed a breath of relief. "Tell him thank you. Can we have a minute with the menus?"

The waiter nodded. "Of course, sir." He turned and left us.

~*~   TT   ~*~

Felicity

This was beyond anything I could have ever imagined. "I can't believe you set this up! This is amazing." The boat was well on its way and rocking gently as we moved forward.

"So you like it?"

"I love it!" Looking around at the other patrons, I grimaced. "I almost feel underdressed compared to everyone else here."

Reaching across the table, I took her hand in mine. "You look incredible. Breathtaking."

Feeling heat rush to my cheeks, I lowered my gaze as a smile spread across my lips. "Thank you for this Carrington. This is like a fairytale."

"I was hoping you'd like it. I may have overshot our first real date though."

"I'm not complaining."

"Not sure how I'm going to top this, to be honest."

"Maybe a trip to Greece? Isn't a European weekend the standard second date?" I teased.

"Damn lady, I'd better get to inking clients. About fifty a day for a month would do it – maybe."

Looking down at the menu, I felt overwhelmed. The food all sounded so fancy and extravagant. After losing the weight, I kept my food preferences fairly basic. Counting calories, fat and carbs had become a lifestyle to the point I didn't even need to record them anymore, I could easily just calculate it in my head as the day went by.

The food on the menu though – I had no clue. But tonight it wouldn't matter. Tonight was about enjoying ourselves and really getting to know each other. I'd already decided I was going to vault my feelings from the past. We were both different people now and while I had hated the boy he was, I was falling hard for the man he'd become.

"So what are you getting, babe?"

Not wanting to look like an idiot, I reached over the table and tapped the entree I was interested in. "What about you?"

"Great minds think alike. That's exactly what I was thinking."

Chapter 13

Felicity

The wine was starting to go to my head as Carrington led me across the deck of the ship towards the bow. The weather had become dreary so most of the other guests vacated the deck of the ship and had went back inside. The music from the band playing inside was also being played from the speakers outside, setting the perfect romantic mood.

Looking at the bow of the ship, I looked up at Carrington. "Hey baby, do you think they'd get mad if I did the whole Titanic thing?"

"You mean sink the ship?" he teased.

Swatting his shoulder, I reached the bow and contemplated climbing to feel the wind in my hair as the ship passed the Statue of Liberty, which was lit up and appearing to glow in the dark on its way back to the docks.

"Don't you get up there," he warned. "If you do, you're getting a spanking when you get down."

I couldn't tell if he was being playful or serious. Taking it that he was being playful, I hoisted myself up, grateful I'd worn heels so I could hook them into the rails and then spread my arms wide. The rail was slightly slippery, but I managed to brace myself well enough that I felt secure. Wind and mist blew over and around me as the ship cut through the water below me. I'm not sure if I've ever felt as free as I did at that moment. All my fears and worries momentarily left me as I indulged in the moment.

"I'm seriously going to spank your ass when we get home. Don't say you weren't warned."

Laughing, I grabbed onto the rails and looked down at him. "If that was supposed to deter me, then you just did a piss poor job of it. If anything, that's just further encouragement."

A low growl rumbled from him as he grabbed me by the waist and pulled me down, slowly lowering me down the length of his body. "You don't listen very well, do you?"

Laughing, I shook my head leaning back against him. "Depends on what I'm being told to do." I felt a surge of desire run through me feeling his hard body pressed against my back. When he wrapped his arms around my waist pulling me tighter, I pressed back against him wiggling my butt against his groin, a smile of satisfaction spreading across my lips hearing him groan in response.

Lowering his face to my neck, he nipped gently, sending a jolt of need through me. "You're a wicked woman. All I've been able to think about over the past few days is being back in you."

I tilted my head to the side, giving him better access to the tender flesh of my neck. "If that's the case, then what are you going to do about it?" The music playing from the speakers was soft and sultry, heightening my arousal.

"When I get you home -"

Grinding my ass back against his cock, I gained satisfaction in feeling it grow against me. "We have to wait until then?"

Chuckling, he nipped at my earlobe. "Then what do you propose?"

The need between my legs intensified as I rocked up against him once more. "It's very romantic here. The music is soft and sensual. It's dark and misty. We're the only ones on the deck…"

His hands slowly slid up from my waist to cup my breasts, each breast fit perfectly in his large hands. Pulling the lace free from the bodice of the dress, he pushed the material aside and slipped his hands under the lace bra I wore. I shuddered at the feeling of his cool, damp hands on my bare breasts. His hands quickly warmed and the shiver quickly turned into a tremble of need as he rolled my nipples between his thumb and index finger turning them into long, tight nubs.

Moaning softly, I rocked back against him again, grinding my ass against his rock-hard dick. "No one will know," I gasped, strangely turned on by the idea of someone seeing us.

The wind picked up, the mist turned into a light rain chilling me and layering my body in cool rainwater. "You might catch a cold." Stepping up closer to me, pressing my body tight against the railing he lightly kicked my feet wider. Releasing my left breast, he slipped his hand to my inner thigh, slowly sliding it up and under my dress, hesitating at the apex between my legs.

"Please," I moaned, my pussy clenching, aching to keep his fingers inside of me.

"Please what?" He ran his tongue along the side of my neck. "Tell me what you want?" His voice was raspy, ridden with lust. Not waiting for me to reply, his fingers grasped the crotch of my panties that were already moist with my need and gave them a tug. The delicate fabric made a ripping sound as he freed me from them and stuffed the torn garment into his pocket.

"Now what?" I bucked back against him again, sliding a hand between us and undid his belt and button to his pants. A few seconds later, his zipper was down, boxers pulled down below his balls and his member sprang free from its restraint.

"Now, I fuck you in front of dozens of people," he growled. "Just remember if we get caught, it's your fault woman." Slipping his hand between my legs again, his fingers spread my labia wide, sliding between the soft folds. His fingers stroked me from my entrance to my clit, pausing at my clit. His fingers worked my clit, sending pulse upon pulse of pleasure through me until my clit was hard and swollen, almost hurting from the intensity of the pleasure.

"Please, Carrington. Please take me!" I cried, worried I may have spoken too loudly, but not caring because what my body needed was more important than whether or not someone saw us.

His torturous fingers released my clit and slid back to the entrance to my pussy. "Are you ready for me baby?" As he asked the question, he thrust two fingers deep into my core, pressing hard against my G-spot and making me cry out. His free hand immediately went to my mouth, covering it. "Shhh. Baby."

His fingers thrust again and a third time, thrusting hard and deep into my core, making me scream out against his hand each time. As I climbed higher and higher towards the summit, I began to rock wildly against his hand. Rocking and moving with his fingers, the pleasure becoming so intense that it'd brought tears to my eyes.

"Please!" I tried to scream out, but his hand kept the plea muffled.

Without further warning, he slipped his fingers from me, pushed my skirt up over my ass and roughly slammed his dick deep into me, knocking my body forward hard against the rail as my pussy stretched to accommodate his girth.

My hands tightened around the rail as he withdrew and slammed into me again as he groaned loudly into my hair. "Damn, you feel so fucking good." Withdrawing he slammed into me a second time, hitting the perfect spot each and every time. The sensations within me building, making my head swirl as I gripped tighter to the rail.

Lowering my head, I moved with him, rocking back against him, meeting each of his thrusts with my own, our bodies working in beautiful unison as though we were two parts of a whole.

As the sensations heightened, I couldn't stop the low moans coming from me, muffled by his hand. The feel of his shaft rocking in and out of me, in combination to the cool, misty breeze teasing my wet pussy and rock hard nipples, sent wave upon wave through me.

The music changed up to a quick tempo. As the beat of the music increased, so did his thrusts, his balls slapping against my pussy with each thrust. Reaching between us, I grasped his balls in my hand, they were hard and ready. Giving them a light squeeze, he groaned loudly and slammed into me so hard, the railing in front of me left me winded, but I barely noticed.

The feel of him releasing his seed into me, the pressure beating against the inner wall of my core, was more than I could handle. I cried out as my core tightened around his dick, milking every last drop of his juice before releasing, my release mixing with his cum deep within me, leaving me gasping and completely spent against the wet railing.

Slowly he pulled from me, the evidence of our lovemaking spilling from me. Before I'd processed what we'd just done, he grabbed my waist again and spun me around, pressing his body against mine and burying his face into my hair. Wrapping my arms around his neck, I held tight to him. I was so close to spilling the words, 'I love you,' it sprang me back to reality.

Just as I'd pulled back from him, I heard footsteps coming towards us. Our eyes locked and he cringed as he quickly tucked himself back into his pants. "You're getting a spanking when we get home, guaranteed now," he grumbled, turning and slipping his arm over my shoulders.

"There you two are. We're going to be docking soon." The captain looked from Carrington's guilty face to mine and back again. "You both seem to be enjoying yourselves, despite the bad weather."

He knew, I saw it in the look in his eyes. There's a chance that he saw the whole thing. I felt both humiliated and completely turned on at the same time.

"Yes, thank you. I appreciate all you've done for us," Carrington replied, squeezing my shoulders.

"Thank you," I parroted, grateful for Carrington's strength next to me. My knees still felt weak from my orgasm. All I wanted to do now was curl up next to him in bed and drift off into a blissful sleep.

Giving us one more look, the captain nodded. "I'm glad you've both enjoyed yourselves." Looking up at Carrington, he added. "I'll give you a call in a few days to book another tattoo appointment if you're open.

"I am."

"Great." Spinning on his heel, he quickly retreated.

Releasing the breath I'd held, I slumped against Carrington. "The shit you get me into."

Looking up, I caught his gaze as he shook his head at me. "I get you into? Pretty sure this was on you. You weren't kidding about being a wild one, huh?"

Chapter 14

Felicity

Snuggling up to Carrington on the sofa felt good and right. I loved the way his body felt stretched out alongside mine. With my head resting on his bare shoulder, I used my index finger to trace the lines of hard muscle in his chest and abdominals.

The night on the boat had been a week ago and it had been an amazing week since. It felt like I was in the middle of a rom-com that one of my clients wrote as though we'd been together for years and I didn't want this high I was feeling to end. All the while, there was a part of me that had an irrational fear that it'd end at any second. I couldn't remember the last time I'd felt so at peace and secure.

The episode of the tattoo competition we were watching ended on a cliffhanger. We wouldn't know until the next week who'd be removed from the competition next week. Turning to face him, I frowned.

Catching my gaze, he smiled down at me. "What?"

"Why don't you have any tattoos?" I'd been genuinely confused about that but had kept forgetting to ask until now.

"I don't know. I just never got one."

"You're a tattoo artist, that's a little odd to give tattoos but never get any."

"I agree. Maybe I'll get someone to ink me eventually when I get a chance."

"What about now?" I teased. "I can hook you up with something wild."

Clucking his tongue off the roof of his mouth, he slowly nodded. "You want to be the first to tattoo me, huh?" Slipping out from under me on the sofa, I groaned my protest reaching for his arm to pull him back down to me but he was too quick slipping out of my reach, causing me to faceplant on the sofa.

"Yeah, I'd be a fantastic tattoo artist," I called after him as he disappeared into his bedroom. "Now get back here so I can get back to cuddling with you."

"In a minute," he called back.

Grabbing the remote, I flipped the channels until I found a sitcom we both enjoyed and switched over to that. We even liked the same silly shows. I tossed the control back onto the coffee table when he emerged from his bedroom carrying a large black hard plastic shelled case. Coming to sit next to me, he placed the case on the coffee table and opened it up, revealing a gun and bottles of ink. Wordlessly, he assembled the gun and prepared the coffee table.

"I have no idea what I'd even want for another tattoo if that's what you're thinking, but I promise as soon as I figure it out, I'll have you do it. You'll do me for a discount though, right?"

"That's not what I'm thinking, smartass."

Sitting up straight on the sofa, I watched him prepare the gun. "Then what are you doing?"

"If you must know, I'm getting the gun ready for you to give me my first tattoo," he said so matter-of-factly I wasn't sure if he was serious or not. Surely, he wasn't serious because there's no way I'd be able to tattoo him.

"Carrington, I have no idea how to tattoo, not to mention zero artistic ability. I'm going to kill your skin and it's going to hurt and it'll end up a mess."

He looked up from what he was doing and smiled. "Maybe you'll be a pro at it." Giving me a wink, he finished up, pushing the leg of his shorts up over his knee, quickly sketching out an image on his lower thigh, just above the knee. It was a simple Celtic cross tattoo design.

"I'm going to screw it up. You really can't be serious."

"As a heart attack."

"Well, I'm going to have a heart attack tattooing you, so that'll be two of us. And if we both have heart attacks, who'll call the ambulance? We'll both die."

Once done with his sketch, he moved and flexed his leg, tilting his head from side to side to get a look at it from all angles. "Yeah, I think that looks good." Looking back at me, he nodded towards his leg. "What do you think?"

"I think you're a fucking nutcase. That's what I think."

"Not the first time I've heard someone say that, but I think it looks good and we're all set. What I want you to do is simply do the outline. Just move the tip of the gun along the lines, it's like tracing lines on a piece of paper. Nothing different than that. Then I can show you how to color it in if we nail the outline."

"You're a madman," I grumbled, taking hold of the gun with shaky hands.

"If your hands keep shaking like that when you tattoo me, it's going to suck." Grasping my shoulders in his hands, he gave them a squeeze. "It's fine. It's not going to hurt much and I'll have something to remember you with."

"Forever."

"Yeah, forever. You're not planning on ditching this relationship anytime soon are ya?"

Laughing, I shook my head. "Not that I'm aware of. Though after I botch this tattoo you might be the one to dump me."

He chuckled. "No faith in me or yourself."

"I just don't want to screw it up, that's all."

"Lucky for me I'm a tattoo artist who works with lots of very talented tattoo artists. Pretty sure no matter how bad you do with the tattoo, it can be fixed if it's atrocious. But I doubt I'd get rid of it even then."

I felt a warmth within me along with the fear that'd encompassed me. He had more confidence in me than I had in myself. He wasn't going to change his mind, the least I could do was give it my all. But there was something else to it. I'd be branding him for the rest of his life. Every time he looked at his leg, the memory of this moment would flash into his mind.

Looking up into his eyes, my heart skipped a beat as time stopped for a moment. I was in love with him, there was no denying it. It was as clear as day and I was pretty sure he felt the same way about me. It felt so surreal, but it was true and as real as the gun in my hand.

It was on the tip of my tongue to say those three little words, but I bit them back. I had a job to do first. Taking in a deep breath, I slowly exhaled and set to work, doing the best I could to follow his instructions.

~*~ TT ~*~

Carrington

I learned very quickly, once she had begun to work on my skin with the tattoo gun, that I needed to make better life choices. Or at least be more selective on who I had do my work from now on. Because… Holy fuck this hurt. She had a very heavy hand, several times gauging my skin as she moved the needle around the outline. I'd have scars on my scars. Every time I flinched from the pain, she'd stab me even worse.

"Shit! Are you okay? You're bleeding pretty bad." She took a disinfectant wipe and wiped away the blood.

Grimacing, I did my best to keep a smile on my face as I shook my head. "No, babe. You're doing great. Maybe just a slightly lighter touch – that's all."

"Okay." She smiled and went back to work, biting at her lower lip as she traced a straight line. She finished the line and lifted the gun eyeballing her work, tilting her head from side to side as she examined her work thus far.

She was about to press the needle into my flesh again when I grabbed her wrist stopping her. "Wait. Let me grab something to drink. One second." Getting up, I hobbled over to the kitchen and grabbed two beers from the fridge. Cracking open the first can, I drank down half the contents before hobbling back to the sofa with the half can along with the full one.

"You're not supposed to drink when getting a tattoo are you?"

"No, I'm not, but it's fine. We're already halfway done." *Thank fucking God!*

"We can stop."

I looked down at the half-done tattoo and shook my head. "No, this is something I want. Keep going."

I really wished I had something to bite down on, it'd taken all my energy to keep from groaning. Maybe tattooing wasn't her calling. It was another fifteen minutes of torture, but she finally straightened with a large smile on her lips and nodded. "Looks good right?"

"Great. You did a wonderful job, babe." Leaning over, I gave her a quick kiss on the lips. "Thank you. Now I can say that I have a tattoo." I motioned to my body. "This canvas is no longer a virgin."

"Righhht." She rolled her eyes and sighed, flopping back onto the sofa, the tension in her body seeming to ease.

"You look exhausted. I was the one being tortured by getting the tattoo you know," I teased, patting her leg.

"That was the problem." She pressed her palms to her chest. "My heart is still beating a mile a minute in my chest!"

Laughing, I grabbed another disinfectant wipe and gently cleaned it up. There were blowouts everywhere and most of the skin was severely agitated from being overworked, but it was done and she was proud of herself, so that was the main thing. Grabbing a square of breathable adhesive tape, I gingerly applied it over the tattoo to keep out any infection and proceeded to clean up the coffee table.

Not all of my ideas were good ones.

"You did well. Maybe tattooing could be your calling if the whole editing thing doesn't work out." I had no idea how I was even able to say that with a straight face.

Her entire face lit up and she bolted upright again. "Oh! That reminds me. I can't believe I forgot to mention this, but my agent got hold of me this morning and the publisher looked over my book again and they passed it on to an associate of theirs. They said they're still not interested as a novel..."

I frowned. "I'm sorry baby, maybe ne-"

She smiled wide, her excitement flashing in her eyes. "It's even better, they want me to fly to L.A for a couple days. They're thinking that it would make a better movie script. They said they could do a Zoom meeting, but they'd prefer I fly down to get to know each other face to face and discuss my future and ideas."

"Wow!" Easing myself back into the sofa, a wave of pride washed over me. "A movie! That's insane. I'm so happy for you."

She placed her hands out, fingers splayed. "It's not for sure yet. It could be nothing, but could be something awesome."

"When do you go?"

She grimaced. "In two days, but I'm only staying for a couple days and then I'll be heading back. Would you want to come? I know it's short notice and all."

"Shiiiit. I Wish I could, but I have a couple clients and I can't turn them down, not when I'm trying to establish myself. I need all the clients and money I can get coming in."

"I understand. I didn't figure you'd be able to." She shrugged. "Thought I'd ask anyhow. It would have been nice to spend a carefree couple days in California with you."

"Next time."

"Exactly." She leaned into me and brushed her lips across mine. "We've got the rest of our lives to travel." Her lips tasted of strawberries from the gloss she liked to put on.

The rest of our lives… I liked the sound of that.

Wrapping my arms around her, I pulled her into me and placed a kiss on the top of her head. She sighed softly, slipping her hand up my chest and to my shoulder. I saw dark hair emerging at her scalp as the blond grew out. "Hey, there's something I've been meaning to ask you."

She lifted her head, her blue eyes which I assumed were brown under the contacts questioning me without saying a word. "What's that?"

"What do you really look like? Without all the make-up and hair color and all that?"

Her body covering mine tensed. Shit.

Chapter 15

Felicity

Damn. I was waiting for that question. I'd been riding the high of our new relationship and had kept the fact we knew each other previously to myself. I knew I should have told him already; I was just caught up in this euphoria that we were riding and didn't want to ruin it.

Sitting up slightly so I could look at him without craning my neck, I ran through what I should tell him. Blowing out a loud huff of air, I shrugged. "Do you have an issue with how I look?"

"No. It's not that at all. I'm just curious. Your natural hair color is dark, I can tell by the roots and I'm pretty sure your eye color is dark as well. I'm just curious. Why don't you stay with what you normally look like? Why change yourself? I'm sure you're stunning without all the extras."

"Should I stop going to the gym and balloon up to three-hundred pounds as well?" I snapped without meaning to.

He recoiled a bit, frowning. "What does your weight have to do with anything? I'm trying to pay you a compliment."

Pushing myself up into a sitting position, I stood in front of him, undid my jeans and pulled them down slightly, pushing the bottom of my tank top up to reveal the stretch marks. We'd never been intimate with the lights on before so I wasn't sure if he'd actually seen them.

"It's because I used to be almost three hundred pounds by the end of high school. That's why I have all those stretch marks. I was fat all through high school. Really fat. I spent my entire high school life being teased for my weight. The torture I endured from other students was relentless. I had no friends and men were never interested in me. I didn't have sex until I was a few years into college."

"That can't be true."

I snorted, shaking my head. He was such a hypocrite. He'd been one of them. "I had dark eyes and long hair. I tried to take care of myself, but no one was interested in the plain fat girl. No guy wanted to be with me, and I struggled to even be the DUFF."

He scrunched his nose up. "DUFF. What the fuck is a DUFF?"

"Designated ugly fat friend. The fat friend groups of girls had to make themselves look and feel hotter."

"That's insane. Girls do that?"

I shrugged. "They certainly weren't all that interested in being friends with me, that was for sure. They were more interested in making fun of me. You'll never know how bad it feels to be tormented because of the way you look. It's so easy to say, just get thin. It's your own fault you're fat and ugly. Or my favorite was – oh you have such a pretty face, if only you weren't fat."

"Felicity." He reached out to me and I stepped away, seating myself at the other end of the sofa as tears filled my eyes. All the taunts and the pain that I kept buried deep within came flooding back to me. I'd done so much and worked so hard to be a different person, yet I couldn't get away from it. I couldn't get away from who I used to be no matter how hard I tried.

"Whoa. Whoa. I didn't mean to upset you, baby." Coming over to my side of the sofa, he attempted to pull me into his arms. I resisted at first, but eventually gave in. Breaking down, I wept freely in his arms. It was the first time I'd completely broken down. I'd kept up a strong façade, hiding my emotions through my transformation. I spent years hiding behind who I wanted to be and trying my best to forget who I was. Then here he comes along, a source of pain from the past rehashing all the feelings I'd tried desperately to keep buried for so many years.

I sniffed, looking up at me and wiping her nose with the back of her hand. "I'm sorry. I didn't mean to get angry. The truth is you wouldn't understand how I've felt all my life. You never will because you were one of the popular, blessed ones."

~*~ TT ~*~

Carrington

Well, fuck. I wasn't expecting that reaction.

My intent was to build her up, not break her down.

What in the hell did she go through for her to break down so badly? Granted, I couldn't relate to how she felt. It had never been an issue for me. I'd never really had issues with other people throughout life. I'd always had friends. I guess you could say that I was popular. I'd always had a group of friends around to lean on and be there when they needed me. Girls were always plentiful.

Truthfully, it wasn't until this point in my life that friends started to drift away. Drifting away maybe wasn't the best way of saying it, more like starting different modes in life. Most were getting married and having kids. While I still had a place in their lives, it wasn't quite the same and not nearly as frequent.

It'd explain why she didn't have older pictures of herself around the place. She didn't like who she was and so she hid it. She didn't have to think about the past she'd moved away from. And like a piece of shit, I'd pulled her back into the most vulnerable of memories.

"I'm sorry." I swiped the tears from her eyes. "I didn't intend to make you upset. I had no idea. Why didn't you tell me this before?"

She huffed. "How would you have known it would upset me? But be honest, if I were three hundred pounds now, would you have dated me? Would you have slept with me? Or would you look at me as just someone who lived under the same roof if you even moved in at all."

"Fuck…" I groaned, running a hand through my hair. I didn't know how to answer that. It was just a crazy hypothetical question. "Baby, I don't know how to answer that. You may or may not be in that situation. I just can't say."

"What if I stopped exercising and gained a hundred and fifty pounds, would you want me then?"

Oh sweet Jesus. There was no way I was getting out of this conversation unscathed.

"Felicity, I want to be with you for who you are. If you gained some weight, then big deal, I wouldn't care. I love your spirit and how smart you are. I love how you appreciate any little thing I do for you and that you believe in me and my art. Your outer beauty is secondary to the things that are more important. How much you weigh doesn't factor in on how much I want to be with you."

"But it would?" she pressed, eyeing me with such scrutiny that it made me shift uncomfortably on the sofa.

I legitimately didn't know. I'd like to think that I'd progressed beyond being the superficial man that I once was. When I was younger, I made judgments and cared what other people thought of me and my appearance. As I grew older, I found I'd cared less and less for those things and more about the quality of the people and things in my life. Admittedly, a good chunk of my progress was attributed to meeting the teary-eyed woman sitting across from me.

"Baby, I don't care what you weigh or what you look like. I just care about being with you. I've only lived with you for a few weeks, but I'm already changing into a better version of the person I once was. I just don't want you to feel like you can't be yourself around me, at all times. You don't need to do your make-up every day. You don't need to put in colored lenses. I don't care about those things and I'd hate to think you'd believe that would matter to me. I just want you to be comfortable and to be yourself – that's all."

Her expression softened and for a moment I thought that I'd finally gotten through to her. Thank God.

"Felicity? Are you okay? Are we okay?"

She chewed at her lower lip as she looked at me. Her make-up smeared, leaving black streaks down her face. "Answer me this."

"Okay…" I wasn't trusting what she was about to ask for an instant.

"Have you ever dated anyone who was larger than me?" She stood again and motioned to her body, from head to toe. "Have you dated anyone bigger? Thicker?"

My heart sank. I had two options here. Either I lie and tell her yes, hopefully ending this here and now, or I tell the truth and face the consequences that I feared might come with my answer.

Taking a deep breath in, I slowly exhaled. "Honestly, no. No, I haven't. It's not that I ruled anyone out… It's just…"

"The type of girl you're actually attracted to. Meaning you wouldn't be with a thick girl. If you were with a fat girl, you wouldn't stay with her." She nodded. "Enough said." Spinning on her heel, she raced across the living room and into her room, slamming the door shut behind her.

"Fuck my life." Groaning, I leaned back on the sofa and closed my eyes. How in the hell did this romantic night, which I felt would end up being a good night with the two of us fucking like rabbits in my room, turn into this shit show. I was so close to telling her I loved her. Then boom!

Looking over at her door, I was tempted to follow her inside, but knew it was no use. She'd have locked the door like she had last time and would refuse to answer no matter how much I tried. All I could do was wait for her to come around and then clear the air once she calmed down.

Chapter 16

Carrington

The apartment felt way too quiet and empty with her gone, leaving just me and Misty. "What do you think, girl?" I asked the dog who was sitting next to me on the sofa while I patted her on the head. We had the television on but weren't really watching it. The movie was a thriller, but I had no idea what was actually going on with it. "You think she's still mad at me? Should we try texting her?"

Felicity had left a day early for L.A. and was due back the day after next. Being apart from her bothered me much more than I'd expected it would. Normally women just came and went. I never gave it much thought or care for that matter. With Felicity it was different. It may have only been a few weeks, but there was something nagging at me. It just felt like I'd known her for some much longer than that.

After she told me about how she'd been bullied in school, something in my head began to turn. I didn't know why but there was a familiarity I couldn't put my finger on. It'd drove me nuts obsessing over it. She'd been right, I had been a vain asshole in the past, but I was confident I wasn't that man now and she needed to know that as well.

I was just about to break down and text her when the phone rang.

It was my mother.

Dammit. If I didn't answer, she'd guilt trip me to no end. With a sigh I answered.

Carrington: Hey Mom.

Janet: Hey Sweetie, how is New York treating you?

Carrington: It's doing pretty good.

Janet: Have you sold any paintings yet?

I cringed. I'd barely touched the canvas since I'd moved in. I'd been so busy with tattooing, I really didn't have much time.

I wished I could relate to how she felt. I just couldn't and would be lying if I said I knew. Maybe if I had a shared experience, I'd be able to understand this side of her, but as it was, I was at a loss of what to do.

Carrington: Not yet Mom. Things are going great at the tattoo shop though.

Janet: Is it? How do you like tattooing? Have you had to tattoo anything weird? I heard there are people wanting their genitals tattooed. Can you imagine?

I could.

Carrington: It's pretty crazy. I seem to be picking it up pretty quick and I've had some repeat customers already.

Janet: That's great. How's your roommate?

Carrington: She's good as far as I know.

Janet: Are you sure you're just roommates? You've never been one to be friends with girls.

I groaned inwardly. She wasn't wrong.

Carrington: She's in California for work right now. I'm watching her dog.

Janet: I'd love to meet her sometime. Maybe bring her home for the weekend some time.

Carrington: We'll see.

My mother rambled on about people I barely knew and had less than zero interest in. Randomly throwing in tidbits that caught barely my attention.

Janet: Before I go, I thought I'd let you know. I was talking to Candice Boyce a bit lately. We've gone for coffee a couple of times. Anyhow, come to find out her daughter lives in New York city now. She has a place in Manhattan actually.

Candice Boyce… The name didn't even sound remotely familiar.

Carrington: Mom, I don't know who that even is.

Janet: Yes, you do. Well, maybe you don't know Candice, but you knew her daughter. I think you two went out for a bit one summer. They lived just a couple of streets down from us.

Carrington: Who was her daughter?

Janet: Connie Boyce. Remember, she had long brown hair… Large girl though. It was unfortunate. She had a very pretty face too bad she was so big. But you two seemed to get along good for a while. Her mother said she lost a lot of weight and was living in New York now. Wonder if she ever found someone, her mother didn't think so.

Time stopped as the pieces quickly began to fall into place. Flashes of the summer I'd spent with Connie came at me, frame upon frame in rapid succession. Her name had been Connie though. Could Connie be Felicity? They had the same surname, so it was quite possible. It'd explain a lot.

Carrington: Hey Mom, do you have contact information for Connie?

Janet: I can get it for you. Do you think you'd like to connect with her?

Carrington: Yeah.

I didn't tell her that I was quite certain that I already had.

Carrington: Listen Mom, I gotta go. Call me later with that info okay?

Janet: Okay dear. Love you.

Carrington: Love you too, Mom.

Ending the call, I looked over at Felicity's closed door. I was already certain she was the same person. There were too many coincidences for her not to be. Not to mention how familiar I felt around her. Even as kids, we'd had a connection that I'd never been able to replicate with anyone else no matter how hard I'd tried.

Pushing off the sofa, I went to the fridge and opened a bottle of beer, taking a long drink as I stared at the closed door. I didn't have any, I had to find out if my suspicions were right. But what if they were?

I didn't know. That would explain her reaction and attitudes towards me. It made more sense than not. But I had to get confirmation before I confronted her. What the fuck, I'd say, and how I felt about the whole situation at the moment was up in the air. I'd figure that out when I got validation.

With my mind made up, I crossed the room and burst through her bedroom door before I'd talked myself out of it. Stopping in the doorway, I surveyed the room. It was very organized and tidy. It'd be easy enough to find what I was looking for if it was here. There was no way she didn't have something from her past. A family photo. A yearbook. Something.

Misty came up next to me, bumping against my thigh. Looking down at her, I grimaced as I stared into her accusing gaze. "I know. But it has to be done."

She groaned a little as she lay down on her stomach in the doorway.

I didn't have a clue where to start so decided on the end tables, not expecting much. Opening the one closest to the side she slept on, I found a diary. Upon opening it I discovered it was a dream diary. Next to it was a big neon pink vibrator – the damned thing was massive. Pulling it out of the drawer, I sat down on the bed and turned it on. The head began to swirl and the little bunny ears began to buzz. How in the fuck did she manage to get this contraption inside of her – it was fucking massive?

Turning it off, I placed it back in the drawer before I started getting an inferiority complex. Some condoms, a pen, some hair ties and a hairbrush. Nothing of any real consequence. Closing the drawer, I went to the other nightside table and came up empty as well.

Turning, I stared at the closet. That's where the photos would be if there were any. Opening the closet, I began to rummage through. The first thing I pulled was a medium sized U-Haul box from the floor. Opening it up, I immediately became amused and aroused. It was a porn star grab box.

Damn! Why didn't she tell me she had all this stuff? There were handcuffs, floggers, masks, butt plugs… You name it and it was there. Her ex was a fucking idiot to give up a sexy little deviant like her. His loss was my gain. Placing everything back in the box, I shoved it back into the closet and pulled out another U-haul box.

This box happened to be exactly what I was looking for. There was a photo album on top along with books and some awards. Stuff you'd normally see on a person's mantel or desk, not tucked away in a box in the closet.

Grabbing the photo album from the box, I was about to flip through it when I spotted the yearbook. The exact yearbook that I'd had when I graduated. Opening it up, there were a few signatures in it, all teachers except for one. I had no idea who the kid that signed it was. Flipping through the graduation photos I looked for the B's and immediately spotted the one I was looking for, Connie Felicity Boyce. She looked nothing like she did now. She'd completely remade herself, but I remembered her.

She'd been one of my first girlfriends. She'd lived a few streets down and we'd been friends in elementary school. When high school started, I'd dumped her and moved on. I wished I could say there was a good reason behind it, but I couldn't. The fact was, I'd been a prick more interested in my own image than her feelings, or my feelings for her, for that matter. I'd been embarrassed that she was so big and to stroke my own ego, I'd dumped her. I'd really messed up with her and had never found anyone who I could relate to until…

I met her for the second time.

"Fuccck…" I hissed the word through my teeth as I sat down on the floor and rummaged through her photo album. There were numerous photos of me and her together. From the looks of it, she hadn't lied. I'd been her only boyfriend until college. There were tons of photos documenting her makeover journey that seemed to take place while she'd attended college. As the weight dropped,the amount of tattoos that covered her body increased, her hair got cut short and went to blond.

Misty whimpered, bringing my attention back to her.

"I'll take you in a few minutes, girl. Okay?"

The dog cocked her head at me and wagged her little stubby tail in response.

"What do I do with this information?" I asked Misty, not expecting an answer. A part of me was furious. She'd lied to me. There's no way she didn't know who I was and yet she kept who she really was from me the entire time. She'd spent the past month avoiding questions about home and her family. I'd suspected her folks were dead or something. Yet, that wasn't the case, she'd intentionally kept who she was from me.

But on the other hand…

I remembered her words from a few days ago. The pain in her voice when she talked about the bullying she'd endured back in high school. I'd been so self-absorbed with what I wanted and trying to impress everyone back then that I didn't try to stop the bullying. I wasn't completely aware of what was happening to her, but I knew she'd been an outcast in school. I should've tried to be her friend at least – if she'd wanted. Instead, I hurt her and tossed her away.

My phone buzzed in my pants pocket. Grabbing the phone, I looked down at it.

Mom: I've got her address.

Carrington: Don't worry about it. I already have it. I'll talk to you later, Mom.

Placing the phone on mute, I shoved it back into my pocket as Misty whimpered a second time. Placing everything back into the box, I slipped it back into the closet just where I'd found it and closed the closet door.

I had some thinking to do. Maybe a long walk with Misty would help me clear my head.

Slipping a pair of shoes on, I grabbed her leash and hooked her up. Leaving the apartment building, we began our walk. We followed Felicity's method of just randomly running until we were ready to go home.

The fact that she hadn't told me raged through me. My mind kept switching from feeling like a complete asshole for what I'd done in the past to anger for how she'd lied to me for so long. She had so many opportunities to tell me the truth. Instead, she spent the last month keeping me on a fucking emotional roller coaster.

Did she have a plan all along? Have me fall in love with her only to fuck with my head and drop me like I'd done to her so many years ago? Could she be that heartless? Maybe she just planned on fucking with me until she was bored?

Stopping at a hot dog cart, I pulled my phone from my pocket and was surprised to see a message from Felicity waiting for me.

Felicity: I was thinking of staying in L.A. for a few more days than expected. Can you watch Misty while I'm gone?

My fingers hovered over the screen, not sure what to reply. I wanted to confront her then and there, but she'd just ignore the texts. I'd rather just surprise her with it. We needed to settle this once and for all.

Carrington: Yeah, no problem.

Felicity: Thank you. I'll let you know when I'm coming home once I know for sure.

Carrington: Sounds good.

Now what? Turning to the hot dog vendor, I ordered two. One with the works for myself and a plain dog for Misty. Sitting on a nearby bench, I slowly ate my dog, while Misty consumed hers in two bites.

By the time I was finished eating, I knew there was no way I could wait for possibly a week to get this sorted out. Bringing up my mother's name on my phone, I sent her a message.

Carrington: Hey Mom, can you find out where Felicity is staying in L.A.? But just let it be casual, don't let her mother know I want to know.

There was a long wait before my mother got back to me.

Mom: That's an odd request. How do you know she's in L.A.?

Carrington: It's a long story, but can you do it, please Mom.

Mom: Of course I can. But I expect the full story once I get you the information.

Carrington: I promise you'll know everything soon.

Chapter 17

Felicity

What in the fuck is with all the damned knocking? Groaning, I slowly opened my eyes and propped my elbows up behind me on the mattress of the slightly too hard queen-sized bed.

"Do not disturb!" I yelled out, flopping back onto the bed. The damned sign must have fallen off the door handle last night. Or someone thought it'd be a fun prank to remove it.

The knocking persisted.

Are you fucking kidding me? I looked over at the little clock radio on the nightstand. It was only 8am! Whoever was on the other side of that door was about to get a word or two from me. What kind of hotel had their cleaning staff knocking on doors this early?

Sitting up, I threw the blankets off me and swung my legs over the side of the bed. Pushing myself from the bed, I made my way across the room to answer the door. I was wearing a pair of Snoopy pajama bottoms and black tank top, so there was no reason for modesty as I pulled back the security lock and opened the door wide.

I opened my mouth to give the person on the other side a piece of my mind, but suddenly lost my voice as I looked up and saw Carrington standing before me, with Misty on a leash on one side of him, a medium-sized suitcase on the other. He looked as handsome as ever, but tired. There were dark circles under his eyes and his hair, which was normally in perfect place, was disheveled.

"Good morning, Connie."

"Carrington… Wh- " Frowning I stared up at him. Did he just call me…

"Would you prefer I continue to call you Felicity or should I just switch back to Connie for old times sake?" He cocked a brow at me, his expression unreadable.

Misty whined, giving her collar a little tug attempting to enter the room.

Stepping back, I allowed the dog and Carrington to enter, closing the door behind them. "How did you find out? Our mothers?"

"Yeah, that's more or less how it went down." Removing the leash from Misty's collar, he placed it on the desk and placed his suitcase just inside the door. Walking over to the bed, he sat down and sighed. "I fucking hate flying overnight."

"When did you leave?" Still confused as to why he was there and unsure of how to feel about it, I sat down next to him. I'd taken some extra time in L.A. to get my thoughts in order, yet the reason I needed time to think was sitting next to me.

"The first flight I could get that I could board Misty on was at 3am. Because it's summer, the airline doesn't like flying dogs in the daytime. I haven't slept yet. The guy in the seat next to me stank, like reeked of sweat and booze. It was disgusting and surprisingly enough, the flight was full so I couldn't swap seats." He ran a hand through his hair. "Who fucking flies at 3am?!"

I shrugged and gave him a lopsided grin. "You do?"

He caught my gaze and grinned. "Fair enough." With a sigh, he stood and stripped off his shirt and jeans.

"Whoa, what are you doing?"

"I'm going to get some sleep. We can fight this out when I wake up, I'm not mentally equipped to go over this whole thing with you while this tired."

I turned my head as he took his thumbs into the waistband of his underwear and pulled them down, kicking them off to the side once they hit the floor and then he proceeded to crawl under the covers. He fell asleep and was snoring the moment his head hit the pillow.

Looking down at Misty, I shrugged. That could have gone a lot worse, though I was left with a lot more questions than answers. "Well, I guess we should get you some water." Grabbing the empty plastic bowl that'd once held a salad and I just hadn't thrown it out, I went into the bathroom, rinsed it out and filled it with water for her, leaving the bowl under the sink in the bathroom. Giving her a pat on the head as she began to drink, I left her to it as I re-entered the bedroom.

I yawned as I looked at the big bed. Screw it. I'd gotten to sleep late and was far from ready to get up yet, so I went to the other side of the bed and slipped under the covers. It took a while to get to sleep knowing he was next to me and unsure of where we stood, but eventually my tiredness got the better of me and I drifted off.

~*~ TT ~*~

The smell of food and the feel of my stomach grumbling woke me from a dream that made no sense whatsoever. Even as I sat up and rubbed the sleep from my eyes, the images had faded, all I could remember was that Carrington had been in the dream.

"Sleeping Beauty has finally awoken!"

My head turned to the left to see Carrington with a room service tray stacked with breakfast foods – pancakes, bacon, eggs, orange juice. "You're here."

And he looked fine as fuck with a t-shirt stretched across his broad chest and a pair of jeans slung low on his waist. I saw the hard lines of muscle under the cotton. Just the sight of him caused a stirring between my legs. It may have been only a few days, but it had been too long since I'd felt him in me.

"I am. Are you feeling okay?"

I quickly remembered him showing up this morning. Oh God, he knew I was actually Connie the Cow. I groaned inwardly. "I'm sorry."

A frown knit his brows. "About what?"

"Lying to you."

"You lied to me?" I could see a hint of a smile on his lips.

My eyes narrowed at him. What kind of game was he playing with me? "Come on, Carrington. You know who I am."

"I do," he confirmed with a nod. "You're Connie Felicity Boyce. We grew up a few streets from each other."

I nodded.

"I also know that I was a pretty fucking big dick to you and part of the reason you had a miserable time in high school."

I nodded a second time.

He passed me a tray containing a glass of orange juice and rounded it with a plate of breakfast foods. "Did you know who I was when I moved in?"

"Not when you applied, I only had your first name, but the moment I saw you I knew. You were my very first boyfriend. Shit, you were the only boyfriend I had until college. You were the most popular kid in our high school, how could I not know who you were?"

"But you didn't tell me."

"Nope." I shrugged. "I didn't know what to think. When I saw you, all the anger and hurt came back. I was going to turn you down and find a different roommate..."

"Why didn't you?" Grabbing a plate identical to mine he sat next to me.

"I don't know. It happened so fast. I needed a roommate and all the applications up until you were duds. I was still bitter with you over everything, but at the same time, I was curious. Then next thing I know your boxes were in the bedroom and you were sleeping in the room across from me."

He stabbed his hash browns and popped a forkful into his mouth. "You had tons of time to tell me the truth. We've been living together for nearly a month. We've spent so many hours together just talking and getting to know each other. There were so many times you could have told me the truth."

"I could have. I just worked so hard at re-inventing myself I didn't want to go back to being Connie the Cow again."

He grimaced, the name visibly hurting him. "Don't call yourself that."

I huffed, rolling my eyes at him. "You didn't mind me being called that when we were teenagers."

"Dammit." Dropping his fork on the plate he sighed, placing a hand at the back of his neck and giving it a gentle squeeze. "Look, Felicity, I was a kid. It wasn't right. I was a prick for what I did to you. I wasn't fully aware of all the teasing you had to endure, I had my own shit going on, but I should've made sure you were okay. We'd been friends as kids and it wouldn't have killed me to be nicer to you as teenagers. I was a piece of shit teen. I have no justification for it. All I can say is that I'm sorry."

"It's all right. It was a decade ago."

"I'm not that person anymore. Neither one of us are those people. We've both grown up and become better versions of ourselves."

"I've struggled with it since you moved it. My emotions have been all over the place. I'd tucked the pain away and not thought about it for years. You coming back into my life made all those feelings come back."

A grin tugged at the corners of his lips. "I'd started to think you had multiple personalities."

Laughing, I nudged his ribs with my elbow. "I guess I sort of do."

"Don't take this the wrong way." He put up a hand to keep me from speaking. "But why all the changes? You literally look like a different person. I kept thinking that I knew you from somewhere, I just couldn't put my finger on it. It'd been eating at me from the moment I moved in."

"Growing up people loved you for who you were. All the girls chased after you. All the guys admired you. Why would you want to be someone else? With me… Growing up was torture. Why would I want to be that person anymore? Why wouldn't I want to distance myself as much as possible from the hurt that came with being Connie the Cow? After I lost the weight, I got rid of the hair color. I wear contacts that change the dull brown that my eyes are. The further my looks got from what I looked like back then, the stronger my confidence became. I motioned to the art on my arms and legs. "The tattoos just took the change a step further. When I look into the mirror, I don't see that scared teenager anymore – at least I hadn't until you moved in."

"I see."

"So where do we go from here?" I waited on bated breath for his reply, hoping now that he'd discovered the truth, it wouldn't change how he felt about me. Wouldn't it be ironic that he wouldn't want to be with me, not because of who I was a decade ago, but because I kept who I'd been from him.

"How about we eat breakfast before it gets cold and then explore the city? I've always wanted to do one of those Hollywood tours. You can tell me how the meeting went while we're out."

"What about Misty?"

"Already taken care of. The hotel has a doggie daycare service, and as long as we're back before 9pm, they'll watch her for a small fee."

"Guess there's no reason to say no."

Giving me a wink, he replied, "Nope, there isn't," before going back to consuming his breakfast.

As much as I wanted to sweep the unpleasantness under the carpet, I had to bring it back up. "What about us though?"

Reaching out to me, he ran his index finger along my jawline. "If you can forgive me for being a prick back then, I can forgive you for nearly turning me into an alcoholic from all the crazy this past month."

Our gazes locked a moment before I burst out laughing, his laughter followed suit. "Okay, it's a deal."

Chapter 18

Carrington

I'd spent the flight to L.A. considering what I'd say to her when I was finally face to face with her. In the end, when it came right down to it, we'd both been in the wrong. Sure, she'd lied about who she was, but I understood. I'd been callus when we were younger and when I'd arrived on her doorstep, it hadn't appeared that anything had changed. It was understandable she'd be hesitant to reveal the truth to me. I could linger on our past mistakes and make us both miserable in the process or I could move on and enjoy the day with her.

The right answer was pretty apparent.

The truth of the matter was, whether it was ten years ago or last week, we'd always had a connection and that never died despite the time and hurt. We'd both made mistakes along the way, but it was time to wipe clean the slate and start over.

"How long are you staying for?" Felicity asked as we walked down Hollywood Boulevard heading towards the Hollywood Walk of Fame.

"I'm leaving on a flight tomorrow afternoon. I could only take a couple days off. Honestly, I shouldn't have taken these off, but I wanted to get things straightened away with you. I wouldn't have been able to concentrate on my work until I did anyhow. Besides, it's not like you've been easy to get hold of."

Her cheeks flushed as she looked down at the sidewalk. "I'm sorry. I was in my head a lot. Trying to sort things out."

"But it's sorted out now?" I gave her hand a gentle squeeze.

"It is." Looking up at me, she wiggled her eyebrows, making me laugh and filling my heart with love for her. "And just think, if we can get past this crazy and slew of misunderstandings, then I think we can get through just about anything."

"Very true. So tell me, what happened with your book?" Even though I hadn't read anything she wrote – fuck I hadn't the foggiest on what it was even about, I had confidence in her. She'd always been smart and determined. That hadn't changed over the years. If anything, it'd become an even more dominant trait in her.

~*~ TT ~*~

Felicity

A bolt of excitement shot through me as I remembered my meeting with the television executives. "I can't believe I didn't tell you! With everything going on between us, I'd completely forgotten. They're going through the entire series. They think it may make a great TV mini-series."

"You're kidding."

I shook my head. "If I'm lying, I'm dying. But it's not for sure yet. Nothing is for sure until the filming begins. My agent feels that it's still a fifty-fifty thing."

"So if it does become a certainty, then how long before we'd get to see your work on the television?"

"Dunno. Couple years maybe."

"Wow, whether it ends up being filmed or not, I'm proud of you baby." Stopping, he pulled me into his arms. Placing his index finger under my chin, he tilted my head up while lowering his lips to meet mine. As our lips met, a wave of emotions waved over me. I leaned into him, pressing my body flush against his, while sliding my hands up and over his shoulders.

The sounds of the people on the street around us faded into the background. All that mattered was him and I and the feeling flowing back and forth between us.

Lifting his lips from mine, he opened his eyes and stared down at me. I saw in his eyes how he felt before he said the words. "I love you, Connie Felicity Boyce." He spoke the words with such dedication and feeling that I didn't even cringe at hearing my real first name. His words were like a warm blanket surrounding me, assuring me that everything would be okay from here on in.

"I love you too," I whispered back. It had been on the tip of my tongue a number of times, but the moment had never been right. But at this moment in time, nothing could have felt more perfect.

When his lips lowered to mine a second time, there was a passion within his kiss that I'd never felt before from him – had never felt before ever. Clutching to him, I moaned against his lips, caught up in the ecstasy of the moment.

When we finally pulled apart, I was left breathing heavily with a deep flush warming my cheeks. "What now?"

"What now is that I take you back to the hotel and make love to you until I have to catch a plane back to New York."

"That's a long time, you're not leaving until tomorrow morning."

"Not long enough if you were to ask me." Stepping back from me, he took my hand and we made our way back to the hotel.

It felt like an eternity before we got back to the hotel room. By the time we were in the room and Carrington had closed the door with the heel of his shoe, my entire body was on fire from the need.

"Do you think we should get Misty first?" I asked, wrapping my legs around his waist as he picked me up onto his hips and carried me over to the bed.

"I'll get her later." Dropping me onto the bed, he kicked off his shoes and pulled his shirt up and over his head tossing it to the floor. "We have a few hours before the doggie daycare closes."

"Even better." I eyed him as he undid his belt, my gaze drinking in every inch of his magnificent body. Focusing on his leg, I grimaced seeing the bandage covering the tattoo. It looked – questionable at best.

"Don't worry about it. It's perfect." Kicking his jeans to the side, he pushed me back onto the bed and came to kneel between my spread legs.

Chuckling, I shook my head. "It looks painful."

"I'll live. I owe you one when we get home." Placing a hand on either side of my head, he lowered his mouth to the side of my neck, kissing and nibbling his way up from my collarbone to my earlobe, sending shivers of desire through me.

"Looking forward to it." Wrapping my arms around his neck and legs around his waist, I pulled him down to me, my skirt hiking up and around my waist. His dick, still constrained by his boxer briefs, buried itself between my legs. I squirmed against him, eager to feel his cock sliding back and forth along my slit.

His lips continued their journey along my jawline and to my lips. "You smell amazing, baby. I don't think I'll ever be able to get enough of you." He ghosted his lips across mine before biting my lower lip.

I moaned softly, the heat between my legs increasing. The thin fabric of my panties became increasingly wet. "Sure a tease."

Chuckling, he moved back down to my collarbone. "I like to think of it as savoring the moment."

I moaned again as his mouth moved across my collarbone to the center of my chest. Slowly, he began to undo the buttons holding the bodice of the pale blue dress together. With the buttons undone, the fabric fell away and my breasts covered in white lace sprang forward. Arching my back, I thrust my chest towards his face, aching to feel his mouth on me.

He undid the front clasp of my bra with a flick of his hand, leaving my breast bare to him. Dipping his head, he nipped at my left nipple. I inhaled sharply as a short burst of pleasure and pain shot through me. Gripping tighter to his shoulders, I moved against his dick, willing it to penetrate past the two layers of fabric.

As he swirled his tongue around my hardening nipple, I slipped my hand between us and under the waistband of his boxers to grasp his dick in my hand. He groaned as he released my nipple and placed a series of light kisses between my breasts to suck the other into his mouth. He repeated the process, nipping at my hardening nipple, sending jolt after jolt of delicious pain.

"Carrington, please," I groaned, pushing his underwear down and springing his dick free. A dollop of pre-cum had formed at the tip which I used to lubricate the shaft, moving my hand up and down his length, feeling it become rock hard in my grasp.

"Soon," he promised, releasing my nipple and capturing my lips again.

His tongue slipped between my parted lips, to duel with mine. As our tongues frolicked, he pulled at my delicate panties. The fabric ripped and the garment came free. "I'll buy you new ones," he promised as he slipped his dick from my hand and slipped it between my folds, rocking back and forth teasing me until I was nearly insane from the desire.

Sliding my hands down his muscular back, I clutched onto his bare ass. Somewhere along the way he'd kicked off his underwear completely. My nails dug into his hard, round ass, my legs tightening around his waist as I urged him to enter me.

He wasn't about to let me off that easily. "Come for me and then I'll give it to you."

I groaned in protest. The fire within me built at a slow and tedious pace,driving me halfway to insanity, making the need of wanting him inside of me too much to bear. "It's torture," I groaned.

Sliding his hand between us, he pinched my clit while thrusting two fingers into me. That act became my undoing. I cried out as I was swept up in the wave of my orgasm. "Good girl." Removing his fingers from me, he traced my lips with the fingers that'd just been inside of me.

I opened my mouth and licked my juices from my fingertips. Once clean, he removed his fingers and replaced them with his tongue, kissing me with a fever that I'd never experienced from him before. I swept away with his kisses as I rocked up against his dick. I wanted more – needed more.

Grasping his dick in my hand, I lined him up and bucked against him, partially embedding him within me. He groaned loudly as he thrust hard, embedding himself the rest of the way – balls deep.

He groaned low and feral, lifting his mouth from mine and looking deep into my eyes. "I can't get enough of you,"

"You've got me for as long as you want me," I whispered up at him as he thrust into me again.

With our gazes locked he moved in me, the motions slow and calculated, the hunger and intense need in his eyes were almost as arousing as the feel of him filling my core. Sliding my hands up his back, I pulled him down to me, his broad chest crushing my breasts beneath me.

My exhale came out as a shutter as I tightened my legs around his waist and held tight to him, moving in sync with his thrusts, our bodies rocking together. His cock moved in and out of me, in slow rhythmic motions as we climbed the mountain of bliss together.

"I've never felt so good," I moaned, placing a string of kisses along his neck. When I reached his earlobe, I whispered, "I love you."

His thrusts paused for a moment as he pulled back just enough to look into my eyes again.

"I love you too," he said.

My heart swelled with emotion. There was so much feeling and sincerity in his voice, it'd brought tears to my eyes.

When his lips came crashing down onto mine one final time, he thrust in earnest. His thrusts, which up until this point had been slow and calculated, suddenly became fast and furious, slamming into me with such force, pushing me deep into the mattress.

The fire within me and between my legs went from simmering to an all out inferno in seconds. I couldn't have kept up with his ferocious thrusts if I wanted to, all I could do was hold tight to him and ride the wave of our passion for each other.

His balls slapping against my ass grew hard, his dick thickening as his body prepared for release. Just the feel of him, knowing he was so close brought me to the edge of the summit, tethering, ready to fall over the edge into oblivion.

Carrington groaned loudly, so loudly I was certain the guests on the other side of the wall heard, before slamming into me a final time. His dick pulsed as it unloaded deep into me. As he ejaculated, his cum filling me to the brink, I went toppling with him. I screamed out, clutching to his shoulders, leaving deep indents into his skin as I came around his shaft.

Feeling his dick unload a second time sent me spiraling yet again. I didn't want this feeling to end but knew I couldn't handle it any more. I shuddered my entire body trembling as I continued to hold tight to him. "Can we stay like this forever," I whispered to him.

"For as long as you want." He lowered his weight down onto my body, keeping himself inside of me.

Forever it would be there.

Chapter 19

Felicity

Carrington was on a flight back to Manhattan and I had a couple days left here in California. I'd already felt empty with him gone and all I wanted to do was go home with him. We'd spent the previous night making love and for the first time in my life, I understood the meaning of the expression "make love." It was on an entirely different level than having sex and I couldn't imagine going back to just having sex now that I knew how amazing it felt with someone who you connected with on all levels – mind, body and soul.

Grabbing a towel from the rack, I stepped out of the shower and wrapped it around me. Seizing a second towel from the rack, I dried my hair. With it being short, it didn't take long to dry.

With my hair dry, I didn't bother with contact lenses. Instead I put on my black rimmed square glasses and gazed at my reflection in the mirror. It was then I realized that I didn't want the blond anymore. I'd worn my hair short and blond for years because I'd been running from who I was, but I was ready now – I was ready to face the person I really was. I was the woman who stared at me in the mirror, but also the chunky, nerdy girl who'd suffered in her teen years. Instead of trying to forget who that girl was, I'd now realized I needed to accept that she'd always be a part of me, regardless of how much I changed my appearance. The scars would always be there and were part of what made me strong.

Leaving the bathroom, I searched for the hotel directory in the nightside table drawer and found the extension for the hair salon in the hotel. Five minutes later, I had an appointment to have my hair done. I didn't want the old Connie back, but there were parts of my old self that I could bring back and it'd start with my hair.

~*~ TT ~*~

Carrington

I gave the table in our apartment another once over, checking over every detail. Everything looked perfect. I had the candles. The lasagna I'd cooked came out perfectly. A bouquet of red roses sat in a vase on the kitchen counter. There was a trail of rose petals from the table to the bedroom and a bottle of her favorite wine chilled in a bucket.

I was certain I'd thought of everything.

The most important part of the night was sitting where her plate would be, in a small black velvet box. It was a big step and so fucking fast, it'd scared me. But it was the right move. There was no doubt in my mind that it was what I wanted and if she rejected me, I seriously doubted I'd ever get past it. She was the one.

Misty was fast asleep on the sofa, unconcerned with what I had planned for the night. How wonderful it must be to be a dog. No worries. No fears. They just get to sleep, eat and enjoy all the treats and love they'd ever want.

My phone buzzed in my jeans pocket. A grin spread across my lips seeing the message was from Felicity.

Felicity: The cab is going to be pulling up to the building in a few minutes. I have a surprise for you.

Carrington: I can't wait. I have a surprise for you too, baby. Love you.

Felicity: Love you too.

There was a point in my life where I was scared of those words, 'I love you'. Now I cherished them. Each time I read a text from her with those words in it, I'd felt a warmth within me that I'd never felt before – it was an intoxicating feeling. Had I been missing out all these years with meaningless one-night stands, or had I subconsciously been waiting for her to come back into my life?

Entering her bedroom, I gave the room one last look to ensure everything was to perfection. It was. I'd exited her bedroom just as she walked in the front door. The moment I saw her, my mouth dropped open and I stood shell-shocked staring across the room at her.

With the door wide open, she stood just inside the threshold. Chewing at her lower lip, she shifted her weight from foot to foot visibly nervous as she awaited my reaction.

Still unable to speak, I crossed the room to her. Her blond hair was gone and in its place was long dark brown hair that fell past her shoulders. I remembered that shade, it was the same shade of brown that it was when we were younger. She wasn't wearing contacts but black-rimmed glasses that gave her a very sexy librarian look highlighting her dark brown eyes. But the kicker was the make-up. Or lack thereof. She was a beautiful woman with the make-up, but without it, she was on an entirely different level. She had such a natural beauty, it was unbelievable to me that she hid it behind the foundation, blush, eyeliner and whatever else women applied in an attempt to make themselves beautiful.

"Okay. Umm… I'm really nervous right now." She threw her hands out at her sides. "So say something. Anything… I might as well be naked right now, I'm feeling that exposed."

"I'm speechless. But in a good way." Reaching out to her, I pressed my palm to her cheek. "My god, you're so beautiful. I'm legitimately at a loss. You were gorgeous the way you were, but this is an entirely different level."

"So, you like it?" A timid smile touched her lips.

"I'm in love with it." I fingered a lock of her hair. "I'm a little confused about the hair. How's it so long? We haven't been apart that long, have we?" I chuckled, watching the strands of hair slip from my fingertips.

"Extensions. I'm stuck with extensions until it grows out on its own."

"So loaner hair?" I teased.

She gave me a sheepish grin. "Pretty much."

"I love it. You look incredible."

Releasing a loud breath of air, she replied, "I feel exposed. Honestly, I do. It's as though all the things I used to do to myself were like my armor."

She looked so vulnerable, it tugged at my heart that she'd let her guard down like that for me. "Thank you."

"For what?" She looked up at me genuinely confused.

"For allowing me to see who you really are. I know how hard it must have been for you."

"I haven't seen myself this way in a very long time. I'm not sure how I feel about it."

"You're going to keep this look? Not that it matters to me, I love all sides of you."

She shrugged. "I'm considering it." Closing the distance between us, she slid her hands up my chest and laced her fingers behind my neck, pressing herself tight against me. "It's only been a couple of days, but I've missed you. Is that crazy?"

"It is. But I feel the same way." Lowering my lips to hers, I gave her a gentle, chaste kiss. "I made supper and I have a surprise for you as well."

Cocking a brow at me, she replied, "Is that so?"

"It is." Stepping away from her, I gave her a light slap on the ass. She giggled and batted my hand away. "Go put your stuff away and I'll serve you supper, you must be starved."

Rushing to the table, I snatched the velvet box up from the table and pocketed it. I wasn't ready for her to see it yet.

~*~ TT ~*~

Felicity

"You made that from scratch? It was great." My stomach was protruding, it felt so full. I'd eaten way more than I should have.

"Thank you. I wanted tonight to be perfect."

"It is," I assured him, reaching across the table and taking his hand. "Carrington, I need to talk to you about something." She popped her shoulder. "Or tell you something. Whatever…"

His smile faded as he eyed me with suspicion. "Your tone is making me uneasy baby. Is everything all right?" He nodded towards the bottle of unopened wine. "Are you sure you don't want any wine? That's your favorite, isn't it?"

Placing my hand over the wine glass, I nodded. He'd gone above and beyond to make this night special. No one had ever gone to such lengths for me before. "It is, but I need to talk to you first." My God, I had no idea how to tell him the news. It could ruin everything.

"Okay…"

There was a silence blanketing the room, the tension between us becoming so thick it could be cut with a knife. I momentarily reconsidered, beginning to chicken out. "Maybe tell me your news first."

He shook his head. "Mine can wait. What's wrong?"

"Okay. Maybe it's better if I just show you." Reaching into the back pocket of my jeans, I removed the long white, plastic stick and passed it across the table to him, my hand shaking slightly.

His jaw went slack as he accepted the pregnancy test. "Is this what I think it is?" He looked down at the positive reading. "Does this mean what I think it means?"

I nodded, holding my breath, praying he wouldn't take the news badly. I was still trying to process the information myself.

"Wow. I think you have my surprise beat, baby." His face went blank. I couldn't decipher a thing from his expression, and it was scaring me shitless.

I released a nervous laugh. "Depends on what yours is."

"Is the baby mine?"

I lifted my brows at him trying to decide if I was angry and insulted by the insinuation or not. "Of course, it is."

He nodded, his mouth remaining a straight line as he stared down at the test. "Yeah, we haven't been exactly careful. Normally, I'm so fucking careful. With us, it just seemed… unnecessary most of the time."

"I never miss my period. Ever. I should have had it a couple days ago. I took the test this morning at the airport before take off. So I'm trying to process this myself. It's still super early and you never know." I shrugged. "I only took the one test so it could be a mistake."

He finally looked up from the test. "Are you okay with this?"

A nervous laugh escaped my lips. "We're already doggie parents, what's a kid added to the equation?"

A smile finally broke out onto his face and he laughed. "Fair enough. We'll take it as we go and if we're parents in nine months, then so be it."

There was another long silence between us.

Taking a deep breath in, he slowly released it. "This makes my surprise even more important." Placing the test onto the center of the table between us, he got up, came to me and lowered himself onto one knee. As he lowered himself, he pulled a tiny ring box from his jeans pocket and opened it.

Gasping, I jerked back in the chair. Of all the surprises in the world, this was not what I was expecting. Not at all, and sure as hell not this quickly.

"Given this new news, I'm even more certain than I was about doing this." Pulling the solitaire ring from the box, he took my hand into his. "I had a whole speech planned, but the fuck if I know what it was I wanted to say now." He looked up into my eyes and I knew all I needed to. "I know I've found my soulmate – again. And I'm determined to not lose you this second time around. Will you marry me?"

He waited for me to reply.

Despite the quickness of this all, I knew there was only one answer. Tears welled up in my eyes as a wide smile spread across my lips. "Yes. Of course."

The tension in his body drained as he placed the box on the table and slipped the ring onto my finger. I stared at the ring for a moment. It felt so odd and surreal that it was happening. It felt as though I was in some sort of dream that I'd eventually awake from or the ending to one of the romance novels that I edit.

But it was far from a dream or a fairytale, this was my life and the gorgeous man getting to his feet before me, hauling me from the chair and pulling me into his arms was my forever.

Epilogue

Felicity

The wedding took place in Manhattan. I wouldn't go back home to Paterson. There was no way in hell I planned on allowing my big day – correction, *our* big day to be jaded by the not so pleasant memories of the past.

Instead, we had a small wedding in Central Park with only our closest friends and family in attendance. It's not like we had much time to plan anyhow. I was already two-thirds of the way through my pregnancy and it was very apparent.

Luck was on our side; it was a warm February day and there was a faint trickling of snow as the ceremony took place. I couldn't have asked for a better setting. Instead of heels, I wore knee high, fur-lined white boots and a fur lined white cloak covering my wedding dress, keeping me decently warm whenever the wind picked up.

Once the ceremony concluded and photos were taken, the wedding party was escorted by horse and buggy to a nearby hotel to have the reception.

Making our way into the conference room the hotel had set up for us, I was taken aback by how good of a job our mothers had done in the room. The colors we'd chosen were red, silver and white. Our parents had run with it and the room looked like a winter wonderland.

"This is amazing, Mom," I said to my mother, shedding my cloak and passing it to one of the waiters to set aside for me.

My mother grinned as she nodded towards Carrington's mom. "I couldn't have done it without Janet's help."

Turning to Carrington's mom, I gave her a hug as well. "Thank you. I appreciate you both." Rubbing my stomach, I grimaced. "I couldn't have done this on my own."

"How has the morning sickness been, dear?" Carrington's mom asked.

"It's been okay." That was a boldfaced lie. It had been miserable. Everything seemed to make me sick. Seafood, popcorn, butter. I was at the point where pretty much the only things I could eat were salads with minimal dressing and muffins. It was strange. I looked up at my husband and slipped my arm around his waist, leaning into him. "Besides, I've had Carrington with me. I don't know what I'd have done without him. He puts up with a lot."

Leaning down he placed a kiss at my temple. "The least I could do."

My mother frowned. "I still think you two should move back to Paterson, we could help with the baby when he or she comes and it's a great community to raise children."

I'd had this conversation with both of our mothers before and was sick of having it. New York was our home now and we wouldn't have it any other way.

Carrington cleared his throat and answered for us. "We can't. I've got clients and Felicity needs to be here as well. Part of her series is going to be shot here in the city this summer. This is where we want to be, but we'll visit and there's nothing stopping either of you from visiting."

They seemed to accept that response, although it wasn't the first time they'd been told this. Our mothers were almost identical in personality. We loved them dearly, but they truly were the stereotypical Karen.

Looking down at me, he added. "Let's go sit down. Everyone is waiting for supper." Escorting me away, we took our place at the head table. My only friend in the city, Alicia and Carrington's boss, Hailey had been my bridesmaids and were already seated by the time we sat down along with his best man.

Once seated I looked over the few tables of our loved ones, including our doggo, Misty, who was laying at the feet of my father. There was a time in my life where I'd felt alone and lost. I'd felt like no one knew or loved me and questioned if there ever would be. Yet here I was surrounded by a small group of amazing people and feeling more love than I'd ever felt in my lifetime.

Leaning into me, Carrington placed a gentle kiss on my temple whispering, "I love you, Mrs. Anderson."

Laughing softly, I looked up into his beautiful eyes. "Love you right back, Mr. Anderson."

Looks like the school nerd managed to score the jock after all.

The End.

To hear about Terry's new releases and upcoming special and promotions, please sign up for her newsletter. Rest assured we will not spam your inbox.

<u>Newsletter Sign-up</u>

Excerpt for

Moist

By

Terry Towers

<u>Available Now</u>

Prologue

10 years ago

Xander

Holy fuck, this had to be one of the most nerve-wracking nights of my life. I was actually getting physically ill thinking about it. I just had to take a deep breath and go through with it. It was even more stressful than making a run for a goal when on the field. At least when I was on the field, I knew what I was doing. This prom night stuff, on the other hand, was a whole new territory.

"Man, I don't know if I'm digging this color."

"I don't think you have a choice," I replied, bringing the black leather dress shoe up to eye level to inspect the shine. It looked pretty good to me. Satisfied, I looked from the shoe to see Keith in front of a mirror scrutinizing himself from every possible angle.

"I should never have allowed Becky to choose pink as her prom dress color." Keith was wearing the standard black tuxedo, but his cummerbund and bow tie was a bright, almost fluorescent pink. It looked pretty outlandish.

"Every guy knows the prom is about the girl. She wanted a florescent pink dress and you couldn't talk her out of it so you're stuck with it dude."

"She was really stubborn about it and she promised she'd do things that we'd never done before if I just went with the color choice."

I grinned. "Then that's your problem dude, you're leading with your dick."

"At least my dick is getting some action."

"Ouch. Fuck man. Hitting me where it hurts, huh?" My grin widened, but the comment stung a little bit.

"Not sure what's the deal with your girl, man. You've been together a year already."

"Yeah. Well, what's worth having is worth waiting for. Tonight's the night. We wanted it to be special."

"Yeah. I think you're just being a sucker. You know there's at least a dozen hot girls in school that wouldn't think twice about giving you a piece of action. You know that right?"

"I do know. But I love Ellie. You know love, it's something you feel about someone else. I know it might be a hard concept for you man, but you should try it sometime."

Keith huffed. "Come on. We're only eighteen. Not even old enough to legally drink for fuck's sake. The last thing we need at our age before we even hit college is to be tied down to one woman. It ain't right. Plenty of time for that when we're out of college."

"Maybe I'm just not built like that. Maybe I like being with one girl – one very beautiful and special girl. Have you seen the photos she takes? She's going to be an amazing photographer one day. Famous even. Just wait and see."

"Great. I'm sure she will, but that isn't getting you action right now though, is it?"

"Well, I don't have to wait much longer. I've got everything all set up. I went to the hotel room earlier and made sure everything was perfect right down to the heart made of rose petals on the bed. It's perfect and she deserves it to be perfect." As much as I wanted to convince him it was all to please Ellie, I also wanted it to be perfect for me. I didn't spend the past five or six years jacking off until I found someone special for nothing.

"Yeah. Sure. Whatever you say."

"Just to point out, I'm the one wearing the blue cummerbund and tie while you're wearing the pink one, so who of the two of us is a punk ass bitch now?" Cocking a brow up at him, I waited for the smart-assed retort.

He huffed. "We will see won't we. I have the room right beside yours. I'd better be hearing some hardcore fucking and moaning going on in your room tonight."

"Sure." Happy with the job I'd done on the shoes, I pulled them on and laced them up. "You about ready? The limo will be here in a few minutes to go pick up the girls."

"Yeah." He gave himself another look and then nodded. Grabbing his suit jacket, he slipped it on. "Handsome as I'll ever be."

Giving Keith a hard look, I had to admit he did look good despite the hot pink. Maybe it was the blond hair and blue eyes that pulled it off. He wasn't quite as tall as I was, but considering I was 6'3 not too many people were. He had that boy next door look that girls seem to flock to and despite my ribbing him, I had to admit he did get the girls. It's like all he had to do was snap his fingers and they came running.

"Passable," I joked.

Grabbing my jacket, I slipped it over my shoulders. Stopping in front of the floor length mirror that Keith had been monopolizing, I gave myself a once over. I was tall and lanky. Ellie said she loved my eyes; she said that she liked how dark blue they were and that they gave me a look of mystery. Running a hand through my dark short hair, I messed with the front to make sure it was perfect before nodding my approval.

I just turned from the mirror when a car horn honked outside.

Our parents were already at the building where the prom was to be held. The school had arranged for the parents to attend the first half hour of the dance so they could get some pictures of their kids and dates before their asses were given the boot. Good luck to them if you ask me. Some parents were fanatical when it came to their kids and getting pictures. Being that Keith and I were on the football team, we got to experience it firsthand. The security would be lucky to get them all out within the first hour.

"Ready buddy?" Keith gave me a jab to the shoulder as he walked past me and towards the front door.

"Ready as I'll ever be," I replied, following behind.

~*~   TT   ~*~

She looked beautiful. Ellie had insisted that I couldn't see her dress until the prom. I'd informed her that was for weddings, not proms, but she stuck to her guns. The only information she gave me was that I had to get royal blue to match her.

I didn't think royal blue could look hot, but I was sorely mistaken. Standing outside of the limo, I watched as she strode down the walkway from her house with Keith's date in tow. My eyes drank in every inch of her from the way her brown hair, which she'd highlighted golden blonde for the prom, shone as the streetlight bounced off it, to the way her breasts pressed against the satin and lace fabric restraining, to the way her hips moved under the tight material that followed her figure all the way down to the ground, fitting her body like a glove. When the wind hit the silver train that flowed out behind her, it added a majestic look to the dress.

As she came closer, the conversation between them stopped and her eyes fixated on me. "Xander! You look so handsome!" She put her hands out and slipped them up my chest as she came in for a hug and brief kiss. The kiss wasn't nearly as long or as passionate as I would have liked, but she was excited and there'd be time for that later in the night.

"You look…" Taking a step back but keeping her within arm's length, I shook my head, releasing a low whistle. "You look incredible. Just… Wow."

Giggling she did a twirl. The wind caught her hair, flipping it up and into her face. "Thank you." Turning her backside to me, she shook her ass a little. "Do you like my train?"

"It's stunning. You're beautiful." Stepping back into her, I wrapped my arms around her waist and pulled her tight to me, inhaling the scent of her apple shampoo. "I've got a surprise for you after the prom."

"You do?" Pulling from my embrace she looked up into my eyes, but there was something a little off about the look in her eyes that I couldn't quite place.

"Come on you two! We're going to be late!" Keith yelled out from inside the car.

Shaking my head to clear the negativity, I took a step back and motioned to the open door. "After you baby."

"Thank you, Sir!" She gave a little curtsey and ducked her head, getting into the car with me following behind her.

~*~ TT ~*~

The prom had started wonderfully. Just like I'd imagined, we danced, hung with friends, had photos taken by our parents, and had an all-around good time. But as things began to wind down, Ellie seemed to grow more distant. It didn't make any sense; this was supposed to be our night together. By the time we were in the car heading to the hotel, I was definitely getting an off vibe from her.

"Are you okay?" I whispered as we sat in the back of the limo across from Keith and his date.

"Of course." She smiled and gently squeezed my hand. "Why wouldn't it be?"

"I don't know. It feels like there's something wrong."

Frowning, she shook her head. "It's fine."

Fuck. The dreaded 'it's fine.' I may only be 18, but I knew that when a woman said 'it's fine' that the situation was anything but. Looking across from us, I quickly averted my eyes. Keith's date was straddling his lap and they were practically fucking. Thank God they still had clothing on. Did he really have to do that right now when we were minutes away from the hotel?

Disgusted, I looked back at Ellie who was looking everywhere but at the make out session across from us. Maybe that was it. It was a big night and with us both being virgins, maybe she had a little jolt of the jitters?

We remained silent until we pulled up to the hotel. The last stop for the night.

Piling out of the limo, we bid the driver a good night and entered the hotel. Keith and I already had our room keys, so we went straight for the elevator. The ride up to the room was taken in silence and by the time we were alone in our room, I knew , without a doubt, there was an issue.

"This is so nice, Xander. Thank you." Kicking off her silver heels she walked over to the desk and picked up the bundle of red roses. Bringing them to her nose, she closed her eyes and inhaled deeply as I watched her chest raise and slowly fall. Opening her eyes, she placed the roses back onto the desk and turned to look at the bed. "This is all too much. I don't know what to say."

Coming up behind her, I wrapped my arms around her waist from behind and nuzzled the side of her neck, just below her earlobe the way she liked. She seemed to respond for a moment, but quickly her body became rigid against mine and she stepped out of my embrace.

When she turned to face me, tears lined her green eyes. "Xander. I think we need to talk."

Wha- What the fuck? Need to talk? Now... On prom night?

My mouth opened to speak, but no words came out.

"Please. Just... Listen. Okay." Taking my hand she led me over to the bed and sat down, patting the bed beside her. "Please."

Feeling numb inside, I sat. "What do you mean we need to talk?"

She inhaled deeply, wringing her hands nervously on her lap. "I haven't known how to tell you this, but I know that I have to tell you this now."

"What now?" Anger began to simmer within me. Why in the fuck was she beating around the bush? How long had she had this thing to tell me, pretending everything was okay?

"Well, we've had plans to attend the same college all through high school and you've gotten into your school. It's awesome. You've got a full scholarship and the whole nine. I'm so proud of you."

"Okay. What's the problem?"

She released a loud huff of air. "Well, I got accepted to a photography school in New York."

"But you're going to school here in California… With me. It's already been done. It's already been set. You got your acceptance."

"I was on the waitlist for New York. I didn't want to tell you because it was such a longshot, but I got in at the last second."

My mind whirled with the information. There were so many questions that needed to be asked. She'd just hit me with a torpedo. "So… We're going to do the long distance thing then?"

A single tear escaped her eye, making its way down her cheek. "Xander… You know I love you, but…"

"But what!" Leaping to my feet, I spun to look down at her. "But what Ellie? I love you and you love me. So we make it work."

"For four years?"

"For as long as it takes!" Raking a hand through my hair, I began to pace. Back and forth from one end of the room to the other, trying to process this surprising turn of events. We had it all planned. I was going to fucking propose on the last day of college. This couldn't be happening.

"We're going to be across the country from each other, Xander. We need to be practical."

I stopped pacing to face her again, doing everything in my power to keep my pain and anger in check. Of all nights to spring this on me. "So what are you saying, Ellie?"

I knew what she was saying, but I wanted to hear it say it. Needed to hear her say it.

She looked down at the floor, beginning to softly tremble. "I think it would be for the best, for both of us if we went our separate ways. We've been together all through high school. I think we need to get out and experience other people. We're kidding ourselves if we think that it'll work long distance for four years."

"Then I'll try to get into a New York school."

"You know it's too late and you've got a scholarship. You can't throw that away for me."

"But I want to."

"I won't let you, Xander." She looked up and I could see the determination in her eyes. She had her mind made up; she'd had it made up for some time. Slowly, she stood and her eyes surveyed the room. "This is so beautiful. I'm so sorry. I felt I needed to tell you before…"

"Before you had sex with someone you don't want to be with?" I supplied, as the anger I tried to suppress came to the surface.

"I just don't want us making a mistake. I just wanted to be honest." She looked back at me, her eyes pleading for me to understand, but I couldn't. I wouldn't.

"I think you should leave Ellie."

"But…" She motioned to the bed. "We can still finish off the night. Maybe not have sex, but this doesn't mean we can't be friends."

As if on cue, soft moaning sounds along with the rapid thumping of a headboard against the wall commenced in the room adjacent to us – Keith's room.

My fists clenched and unclenched at my sides. *You've got to be kidding me.* It was like salt being thrown onto the wound. The need to grab something and throw it was becoming unbearable. It took everything I had in me to keep my emotions under control.

"Leave Ellie. Leave now." When she didn't respond, I cursed under my breath and stormed past her. "Never mind, I'll leave. Happy fucking graduation." The nastiness in my voice was so strong that it even made me grimace as I opened the door, slamming it closed behind me with such force that the picture mounted on the wall next to the door in the hallway rattled.

Love. It's a fucking crock of shit.

Well, never again.

Never again will I allow a woman to do to me what Ellie just did.

Never the fuck again!

Chapter 1

Xander

Damn. What a night.

Groaning, I carefully slipped my arm from under Becky's head, hoping not to wake her... Was it Becky? Maybe it was Brittney? Fuck it. Did it really matter? Slowly, I rolled over to my back and stretched, groaning a second time as the kinks and knots loosened in my lower back and legs.

Grabbing my phone from the nightside table, I turned it on and looked at the time. 8am. I'd had 4 hours of sleep tops. No wonder I was still fucking tired, the show last night had been wild and the one-on-one after party with the girl beside me had been vigorous.

But it was time to get up. I had work to do before tonight's show. Saturday night was always the busiest night at the club and from my understanding, the owner of the strip joint that I danced at had a large bachelorette party coming. One of the girls in the group was supposed to be our photographer for the yearly calendar so he wanted her to get a feel for each of the guys in our group.

Whatever. A show was a show. It's not like I could thrust my hips any harder than I normally did during our lap dances or I'd pull something. But I could at least be rested up so I didn't look twice as old as I really am.

Sliding from the bed, I gathered my clothing and quickly threw them on. I was at her place, a small one-bedroom apartment just off the strip. It was cute but was much too claustrophobic for my liking. She had a lot of stuff and just not enough room to store it all, so it resulted in lots of clutter.

Crossing the living room, I entered the little kitchen and opened the fridge. Grabbing the carton of milk, I searched the cupboards until I found a glass and poured myself a full glass, drinking it down. Through my search for a glass, I came upon a box of pancake mix.

Remembering I'd seen a container of blueberries in the fridge, I grabbed them and began to whip up a batch of blueberry pancakes large enough for both myself and the girl in the bedroom, while I waited for the skillet to heat up to the optimal temperature. While I waited on the skillet, I noticed some mail in a little metal magnetic holder on the side of the fridge. The name on the mail was Sonya Caine. Fuck, I was totally off on the name.

Guessing the skillet was heated up well enough, I poured a little of the mixture in the pan and waited on my test pancake to cook. It seemed to turn out decently enough so I poured enough for several more pancakes. I was nearly done with the batch when I heard her stirring in the bedroom. Moments later, she appeared with an oversized t-shirt on that I guess may have belonged to an ex, with her brown hair dishevelled and rubbing the sleep from her eyes.

"Good morning Sonya, baby. How was your sleep?" I greeted with a smile on my face as I scooped up the last of the pancakes, placing them on the platter with the rest.

"Excuse me?" She went from barely functional to fully awake in an instant.

"Oh." I looked down at the pancakes and cringed. "I'm sorry. I took the liberty of making us breakfast. I didn't think you'd mind."

"No, I mean." Her eyes narrowed and she stalked towards me as if I were prey. "What did you just call me?"

"Baby? Is that a problem? I didn't mean to offend you."

"No." Her dark eyes flashed with annoyance. "I mean my name. What did you call me?"

Grimacing, I looked back at the mail. It did indeed say Sonya. "I'm confused."

"My name is Becky. NOT Sonya."

"Ahhh." My brow creased. "I…"

"You don't even know my fucking name!"

"Wait." Placed the spatula on the countertop, I put my hands up in surrender and slowly backed away as she stalked closer to me. "I'm genuinely confused."

"What do I do for a living, Xander?" She grabbed the spatula I'd just set down, waving it at me. Not sure what she planned on doing with that spatula, but I suspected that getting kinky in the bedroom wasn't it.

"I…" I had no fucking idea. It was worse than the name situation. Backing up a little more, I made my way to the door and my shoes.

"Get the fuck out of my house, Xander!"

"Whoa, wait. Just… I'm not great with details and in my defense we just met last night. It's not like we did much talking."

That's when the spatula came sailing at my head. Her aim was terrible, not even coming close to hitting me. "Get out!"

"But I made you good morning blueberry pancakes. That should account for something, shouldn't it?" Granted I made them because I was hungry, she'd been an afterthought. I protested, putting on my sneakers as quickly as possible not expecting that argument to sway her.

"If you don't get out of my house, I'll shove those pancakes up your ass!"

"Fine. Okay." Grabbing the door handle, I opened the door and started to leave but hesitated a moment. "One question?"

She stood perhaps ten feet from the door, her hands planted firmly on her hips as she glared at me. "What?"

"Who's Sonya?" The moment I noticed her go for another kitchen utensil I knew I'd overstayed my welcome and there was no coming back from the fuckfest I'd just made of the morning. Ducking out the door, I closed it behind me and sighed a breath of relief as I leaned back against it. Lesson learned, don't assume a woman's mail is hers.

Pushing myself off the door, I made my way down the stairs and into the parking lot. Visitor parking was way the fuck at the back of the parking lot, so it took me several minutes to finally get to my Jeep. My black 4-door Jeep Wrangler was my pride and joy, fully customized to my likings. I'd saved and bought it in cash, but now I had bigger fish to fry. I was now saving for my dream, it's just that my dream was much more expensive than a Jeep. Which is why I worked two jobs. The beauty of Las Vegas was that there was always employment to be had if you were willing to work hard.

Getting into the Jeep, I pulled the keys from my jeans pocket and thrust them into the ignition, bringing the vehicle to life. My stomach grumbled as I backed the Jeep out of the parking spot and flashes of the pancakes came to my mind. Damn they would have been good.

No matter. I'd go home. Get some food. Maybe a nap. Shower and then off to job number one for the evening.

~*~   TT   ~*~

Shawn's brewery and bar was nice and peaceful compared to the strip club. It was busy, don't get me wrong on that, it featured beer from all over the world and was actually a destination spot for Las Vegas tourists, most of which were happy to be here and tipped well for their drinks. But what set it apart was the fact there weren't masses of screaming, plastered women trying to catch a feel of whatever body part came within reach.

Having been to a man's strip club and then working for a woman's club, I can tell you right now that women were by far the rowdier of the two sexes. While men generally kept their hands to themselves knowing the rules and knowing if they did get to hands on that they'd get their asses kicked by security; on the flip side women touched, grabbed and caressed every part they could. There wasn't a night that went by that I didn't get my junk groped at least five times a night.

But I digress… It was part of the job. And the job paid well so I wasn't about to complain too much about it. Besides, it was all a means to an end. That was all.

"I really wish you could stay later tonight Xander," my boss and owner of the bar said, filling up several glasses with the newly released brew. "We're getting slammed."

I grimaced. "I'm sorry. I really am. But I've got to perform tonight. Saturday night's are insane and the boss has a big party coming in."

"And the money is better."

A smile touched my lips as heat lightly colored my cheeks. "That too. You know I have a plan and I'm getting closer by the day. With any luck I'll have enough money saved to start my own brewery very soon. It'll be small, but it'll be mine."

"Yeah, yeah. Come here. Work with me for five years and then leave with all the brewing knowledge that I've bestowed upon you, my young grasshopper, to become my competition." He shook his head and scowled, but I knew he was just joking. We'd become great friends over the years, and he rooted for me almost as much as I was rooting for myself.

"I'll give you a healthy discount on the beer I produce."

"Boy, thanks. I appreciate that." Shawn said dryly, turning from me and serving the glasses to the customers waiting for them.

"Anything else I can get ya?" I asked, sliding the glass of beer I'd poured across the bar to the pretty young woman on the other side. Her dark eyes looked down and then back up, and she batted her lashes at me. "Maybe I can see you tonight? After you get off work?"

Chuckling, I leaned forward catching her gaze. "I don't get off for a while."

"I'm patient." She slipped a long black lock over her shoulder.

"Well, if you really want to see me after I'm done here..." Straightening, I reached in my back pocket and pulled out a business card for the club, Moist, that I stripped at. "You can head on over to the club I work at. When you've got your fill with the brew here. The brew here is far superior to the generic shit they serve there. Though they do have a few craft brews in now, I think."

Her eyes widened. "You're a stripper?"

Taking another step back, I motioned to my body clad in a pair of jeans and a tight fitting, black ribbed t-shirt and winked. "Exotic dancer, baby. Gotta get it right."

"When do you go on? Tonight?"

I nodded. "Show's at 9pm and 11pm." Wagging a finger at her I added, "Better see you and your friends there."

She nodded. "You sure will."

"Pouching my customers as well," Shawn joked.

"I'll send them on back after the show with all their friends." Giving my boss and friend a slap on the back, I added, "Now I have to run. I'll try to get back to help out before closing." The bar and club were only a couple blocks from each other so when I hurried, I could sometimes help out for an hour or two before we shut the brewery down for the night.

Terry Towers

Contact Information and Release List

Email: terrytowers@hotmail.ca

Facebook Page:

Facebook Profile:

Amazon Author Page

Twitter:

Instagram:

Pinterest:

Amazon Books

Ménage

Two Times the Mountain Men

Her Untamed Rockstars

The Brother's Next Door

Her Twin Stepbrothers

Strictly Research

Forbidden Indulgences

What Happens In Vegas… Doesn't Always Stay There

Ride a Cowboy… or Two

Coffee Shop Series

The Cop and the Girl from the Coffee Shop

The Politician and the Girl from the Coffee Shop

The Assassin and the Girl from the Coffee Shop

The Bounty Hunter and the Girl from the Coffee Shop

The Firefighter and the Girl from the Coffee Shop

The Porn Star and the Girl from the Coffee Shop

The Tattoo Artist and the Girl from the Coffee Shop

The CEO and the Girl from the Coffee Shop

The CEO and the Girl from the Coffee shop 2: The Pleasure in Surrender

The Rockstar and the Girl from the Coffee Shop

The Rockstar and the Girl from the Coffee Shop 2: Under Pressure

Dark Romance

Trust

Faith

Freed

Obsessed

The Hitman's Secret Love Child

Taming a Dark Heart

Moan for Him (Complete Forbidden Series)

The Rivalry (Complete 3 story series)

Stepbrother's Unbridled Passion Boxed Set

Behind Closed Doors

Naughty but Nice Bundle

Crossing the Line: Forbidden Love Boxed Set

Multi-Author Boxed Sets

Our Little Secret (10 Story Taboo Boxed Set)

Red Hot and Taboo Boxed Set (8 Story bundle)

Pushing Boundaries: Dominant Male Boxed Set (8 story bundle)

Alpha Men in Authority Boxed Set

His to Control Boxed Set

Forbidden and Taboo Love Boxed Set